Hell o. _ ..

Crypt Witch cozy paranormal mystery
series - book 2

K.E. O'Connor

K.E. O'Connor Books

HELL OF A WITCH

ISBN: 978-1-915378-00-2

Written by: K.E. O'Connor

Chapter 1

It was official; I hated the city. Not this particular city but all cities. And crowds, not a fan of those either. As I shoved my way through the throng of non-magicals turning out from their office jobs, I made sure to keep my breathing shallow. The smell of stale coffee and what might have been desperation wafted off people's clothes as I passed them.

The fumes from the vehicles crawling by almost made me gag. I'd never considered myself a country girl, but every time I came to a city like this, I changed my mind. What I wouldn't do for a lungful of clean, fresh air from Willow Tree Falls and only the occasional buzz of a bike or car dawdling past me. This stress-fueled, horn honking misery did nothing for me.

I stepped to the side to get out of the worst of the commuter foot traffic and reluctantly took a deep breath. I filtered out the stench of the non-magicals around me. I was seeking one smell. The stench of a demon. Every demon came with an unpleasant whiff of sulfur. Some were worse than others, like they'd spent their morning bathing in a bucket of rancid eggs. This one was your average smelly demon. Raksh was a sneaky one, though. He'd eluded me for three long, city stinking days.

I blamed Angel Force for giving him such a good head start. Dazielle hadn't told me he'd eluded their custody until almost a week had passed. His head start caused me more of a headache than I needed. Not that I needed another one.

My nose wrinkled, and I stepped into the alleyway on my left. I was running this gig solo. Before Wiggles had turned into a hellhound, he'd often accompanied me away from the magical bubble of Willow Tree Falls on the demon hunts. He was good at finding demons when he wasn't distracted by food. And it was nice to have company, especially in the world of non-magicals, where everything felt a little off and weird.

Since Wiggles' transformation, he was confined to Willow Tree Falls forever, unless I could figure out a way to maintain his magic away from the sanctity of our home. He didn't seem to mind; he loved Willow Tree Falls, but I did miss hanging out with him.

No matter, I had a demon to hunt in an alleyway, and time was not on my side. I'd already had three urgent messages from Mom on my mobile snow globe, reminding me in an increasingly shrill tone that I needed to get back in time for the mid-summer solstice celebrations that evening. It was a big deal in Willow Tree Falls. Solstice was a time when we recharged our magic batteries and gave thanks to the power at our fingertips, a power that none of the non-magicals around me knew anything about.

That was why I was creeping along a grimy alleyway. I was searching for this demon to keep the non-magicals safe. I sometimes wondered why I bothered to risk my neck to keep their eyes shielded from the magic truth. Every non-magical I met seemed unhappy. When they came to our healing stones or to try our thermal spas, it was in the hope of a restorative cure for their stress aches. If they knew what really lurked around many a dark corner, they'd be even more stressed.

The noise of the busy street faded as I continued along the alleyway.

"Here demon," I whispered. "Come take a nap in my cute little bag." I patted the plain brown bag that hung from a belt loop on my black pants. This wasn't your normal bag; there was no make-up or hair spray in here. This bag was a miniature demon prison, just like the one my family looked after in the cemetery at Willow Tree Falls. The Crypt family was in the business of demon hunting and incarceration and had been for centuries.

My bag had nothing on the prison, but could hold a demon as I transported him to Willow Tree Falls and let the angels determine the fate of the demon I'd captured.

My sister, Aurora, was always trying to make it pretty by attaching pin badges and sticking on sequins. They never lasted. Demons hated the bag. They fought tooth and claw to avoid being shoved into it, and all the pretty stuff fell off.

The sulfurous smell grew. I glanced up at the grimy brick walls surrounding me. Nope, no demon hiding there waiting to pounce on my head. Raksh was a shapeshifter and could fly short distances. All demons had the potential to live forever if they looked after themselves. Raksh was several hundred years old and wanted for three ritualized sacrifices of non-magicals. In his defense, he'd said he needed to conduct the rituals to maintain his strength, given that so few non-magicals worshipped him anymore. But he'd broken magic laws. We never harmed non-magicals, unless they directly threatened us, no matter how annoying they could be with their giant purses and obsession with cell phones.

A door slammed open behind me. I spun on my heel, the bag raised, ready to capture Raksh.

A red-faced man wearing a white apron slung two black bags of trash out the door. He glanced in my direction, and his eyes widened. "What are you doing out here?"

"Enjoying the view." I lowered the bag and acted like it was my right to be lurking around a dark, damp alley.

"You shouldn't be back here."

I shrugged and looked away. I hoped this guy wouldn't give me trouble. There was a demon around here, and the non-magical wouldn't want to be anywhere near us if we fought. Demons liked to use non-magicals as shields.

The guy snorted before pulling the door shut behind him, muttering something about junkies and ending up dead in the gutter.

"As if," I said quietly to myself. The kind of drugs they served in the non-magical world held no appeal. Now, if you placed a bowl of my own home-dried magic mushrooms and a few lemon drops in front of me, I'd be tempted.

I scratched my way through some trash, grimacing as I did so. A hot swell of Frank's energy shifted up my spine as if he sensed danger. Frank, my unwelcome resident demon, was my constant companion, no matter what I tried to get him evicted. Having swallowed him to save my sister when we were kids, he now lived inside me but often tried to get out and finish what he'd started with Aurora. He also didn't react well to stress or danger, something I often found myself in.

"You can stay where you are," I muttered to him. "I'm dealing with this one."

He chuckled quietly but made no further attempt to get out.

I'd given Frank a couple of hours respite as soon as I'd left Willow Tree Falls and was a safe distance from my family. He had to come out now and again; otherwise, my resistance weakened, and he could take control whenever he wanted.

I remembered little about those hours and had woken with a banging headache, the taste of whiskey on my breath, and the remains of two takeout pizza boxes beside me. Who'd have thought demons were junk food addicts? And Frank had the sweetest tooth imaginable.

I glanced down at whatever disgusting thing I stepped on as it squelched beneath my black boot. It might have once been a used diaper.

When I looked up, a long-limbed, green-scaled demon stood in front of me, his pinprick sharp teeth bared. I shook my head. Why couldn't Raksh have shape-shifted into something cute, like a unicorn or a fluffy kitten? Why did it always have to be something gross and scaly, something with teeth and long jagged-looking claws?

I opened my bag. "I hope you're going to come quietly."

Raksh hissed and swiped his claws at me.

"I take that as a no."

Raksh inclined his head. "I am honored that a Crypt witch would come for me."

"Don't be. I was the only one with free time on my hands."

Raksh chuckled. "I know you, Tempest Crypt. You work for the angels."

"I work for myself." It always grated that I freelanced for Angel Force. If they only knew how to do their jobs properly, I wouldn't have to go running around clearing up their mistakes. But my family insisted we help them. It was an old tradition, starting back in the days when my Granny Dottie dated the old Angel Force police chief. Even though he was retired, she still felt we needed to give them a hand and capture all the mad, bad demons who escaped their clutches more regularly than they should.

The demon capturing fell to me if it happened outside of Willow Tree Falls. The rest of my family spent their time guarding the prison and kicking any demon butt that decided to sneak out.

"You're a pretty witch," Raksh said. "I'd like to wrap my claws into your long hair and take a bite of that creamy skin."

"If you're hungry, there's a pizza parlor a block away."

"I prefer my food alive when I eat it." His forked tongue flickered across his teeth.

I shrugged. I'd met worse demons. I lived every day with a worse demon inside of me. Raksh could issue all the threats he wanted, but this demon was going in my bag. There was no way I'd miss the mid-summer celebrations because of this rule breaker. The celebrations meant lots of home-baked goodies and partying, and I was always down for some of that.

Plus, my own business, Cloven Hoof, was hosting a stall and selling pick me ups and tonics to give everyone a little extra buzz. My bar manager, Merrie, would cover the stall, but when Willow Tree Falls was full of celebrating locals and non-magicals, she'd need all the help she could get. I promised her I'd be back in time.

Raksh twisted his neck unnaturally. "How about we play a game?"

"I don't have time for games."

"How about I guess the real name of your demon?"

My breath hitched. No one knew Frank's real name. To know a demon's true name was to have power over him. It didn't mean you could completely control the demon, but it gave you leverage and weakened them. I'd deliberately chosen the name Frank for my unwanted guest because it sounded like such a harmless name, and I knew it annoyed him.

"I see I have your attention." Raksh tapped his claws on the brick wall.

"You can't know who he is," I said. "Nobody does."

"Some do. Your demon does."

"He's not going to tell me, and I doubt the two of you ran in the same circles when he was free."

Raksh shrugged. "If you're not interested—"

"I didn't say that. What do you know?"

His sharp-toothed smile grew. "Lower your bag, take me for a pizza, and we'll talk."

This was a con. It had to be. Still, I was tempted. If I knew Frank's real name, it would make my life so much easier. I'd be able to spend more time in Willow Tree Falls with my family. As much as they annoyed me at times, I still loved them. It hurt to have to leave in order to keep them, and Aurora in particular, safe.

"I'll buy you one slice, and you tell me everything you know about Frank."

"I want a family-sized stuffed crust with twelve toppings. And I want dessert."

"Two slices."

"A medium Margherita with a stuffed crust."

"A small Margherita and no dessert."

Raksh scowled at me. "Very well."

The door behind me opened again. Two guys stepped out with cigarettes in their mouths.

The demon lunged at them, screaming in an ear splittingly high range as he did so.

"Oh, balls!" I threw myself in front of the two men. Raksh would try to injure the non-magicals in the hope he could slip away in the chaos.

"What the…" One of the men jumped backward, and his cigarette landed on the ground.

Demons could reveal themselves to non-magicals, but they usually only saw a blur of movement when a demon was around.

"There's nothing to see here," I yelled. "Get back inside." I took the full force of Raksh's charge and stumbled into the non-magicals as his energy slammed into me.

Raksh bounced away, his laugh echoing off the walls.

I felt hands on my shoulders and quickly shrugged them off. "Get inside. It's not safe out here."

"Are you a cop?" one of the non-magicals asked as he scanned the alley with wide eyes. "Is something going down out here? Bruce said there was some junkie hanging around in the alley and to be careful when we came out for a smoke."

"Bruce would be right. I'm much worse than the cops." I blasted a throwback spell into Raksh's chest as he dove at me, giving me a few seconds before he launched himself at the non-magicals again.

"What did you just do?" The taller of the two non-magicals stared at me with his mouth open.

"Nothing. It was a camera flash. I'm collecting evidence of the junkie. Now, get inside." I gestured at the door. Why weren't they getting the hint? They'd be dead if they didn't get their butts out of this alley.

"Are you sure we can't give you a hand? You look kind of small to handle some doped-up loser."

"I can handle plenty more than that. Let me help you find the door." I grabbed hold of them by the collars of their work shirts and threw them through the doorway, slamming it behind them and sealing it with a spell.

As I turned back to face Raksh, he threw himself at me. There was no time to open the bag as his claws flashed in front of my eyes.

I took a breath, steeled myself for what was about to happen, and swallowed him. He struggled and spat curses at me. He also exuded a sour tasting green goo that had me using all my willpower so as not to spit him out.

Tears ran down my cheeks as the hot acid sensation of a demon sliding down my throat tore through me. It was never my preferred method of capturing a demon. The bag was so much kinder on my stomach. This was a rare gift of mine, if you can call it a gift, being able to contain a demon inside me.

A loud belch shot out of my lips. That was another side effect of hosting demons. I almost lost my grip on Raksh. It didn't help that Frank was already inside me and occupying so much space. He did not like to share his living accommodation with anyone.

"Stay down," I muttered as I gripped my stomach and leaned against the wall, feeling the demon's power trickle through my body, the hot energy heating me from head to toe.

After several minutes of deep breathing, I had Raksh under my control and a gross coating of green demon goo all over my favorite black shirt and sliding down my chin.

"There she is," came a shout from the end of the alleyway.

I looked up to see two cops staring at me. The guys I'd shoved through the door stood next to them.

"She's the junkie who attacked us."

"Thanks for nothing, guys. Next time, I'll let the demon play with you." I pushed myself away from the wall. It was time to leave. I'd gotten what I needed, but this had been a messy search and retrieval operation. Whenever possible, we didn't use magic around non-magicals. It left them confused and reporting they'd seen some alien or a ghost to a tabloid paper.

I was out of options and trapped in an alleyway with two cautious looking cops heading my way, their hands too close to their guns for my liking. I also had two restless demons on board. I had about two hours before I lost control of them both. I had to get back to

Willow Tree Falls and release Raksh. I needed to use magic again.

I focused my energy on a transportation spell. This was taxing magic, so I needed to concentrate.

"Miss, what are you doing in this alleyway?"

I ignored the cop and imagined stepping through a door and finding myself on the main street in Willow Tree Falls, seeing the pastel pink sign of Sprinkles bakery and Wiggles racing toward me with his tongue hanging out.

"Miss, place your hands where we can see them and walk toward us."

I shook my head, closed my eyes, took a deep breath, and stepped forward.

Chapter 2

I let out a relieved sigh as I opened my eyes and found myself in Willow Tree Falls. The cops would have a great story to tell their friends at the bar tonight about a goo-covered woman, who had vanished into thin air. Not that I cared about that; no one would believe them. But the world was down one demon thanks to my capture of Raksh. It was a win all around.

I felt the ground tremble beneath my feet and had just enough time to catch Wiggles as he launched himself into my arms. I collapsed backward on the ground as his furry face crowded mine and he licked my cheek.

"Have you missed me?" he asked as he continued to give my face lots of affectionate, sloppy licks. "You taste gross by the way, and you're covered in slime."

"Thanks for nothing." I ruffled his fur, rolled him off me, and stood. "I've been stuck in hell for three days and am carrying two demons. I'm going to taste gross."

Wiggles tipped his head to the side. "You didn't bag him?"

"Raksh didn't want to be bagged. He wanted to eat some non-magicals, so I had to think on my feet." I brushed dust off my black pants and stopped to check out Wiggles properly. "What are you wearing?"

Wiggles sported a jaunty-looking red bowtie and matching collar.

He snorted. "It's your sister's idea. She thinks everyone needs to dress up for the celebrations."

"You chose a bowtie?"

"She chose the bowtie. Aurora said it made me look dapper."

"It makes you look something." I hugged Wiggles, glad to be back in Willow Tree Falls and surrounded by everything I loved.

He endured the hug for a few seconds before wriggling out of my grip. He was less cuddly now he was a hellhound. I tried not to take it personally.

"What do you say we go sample the goodies?" he asked. "Some stalls have already set up, but the main event isn't kicking off for a couple of hours."

I looked around as people wandered past us. I got a few curious looks, but it wasn't so unusual to see me covered in demon residue and dirt. "I should clean up and offload this demon on Angel Force before we party."

"Five minutes of eating cake and partying isn't going to do you any harm. Every demon loves cake, so Raksh isn't going to mind you stalling his imprisonment for a bit." Wiggles bounded around my feet.

I sniffed the air and smiled. "Has Patti got her stall out?"

"Sprinkles' stall is all ready to go. And she's giving away free samples. I spent the last half an hour being chased off by her after I stole a plate full of chocolate tiffin."

"Mmmmmm, chocolate tiffin." I looked along the main street. "Five minutes of fun won't hurt."

Wiggles nodded. "Decision made. It's party time."

An hour and a half later, I had a giant food baby in my stomach from too much cake and was feeling queasy. I sipped on my lemon water as I watched Wiggles run along beside a pretty little tan bitch. It looked like he was flirting with her.

Tilly Machello, owner of Bite Me, sat in the seat next to me. "It's nice to have you back. I'm guessing from your state that you had a successful trip?"

I patted my round stomach. "The demon is happily on board." I stifled a belch. "Well, maybe he's not all that happy, but he's not getting out."

"I thought you had an interesting smell about you," Tilly said.

I sniffed my sleeve and grimaced. "I blame the demon goo."

"Me too. That's always my story." She grinned at me. "It's going to be a busy one tonight. I've got two dinner sittings booked, and there's the stall to run. Any chance you can give me a hand?"

"Not a chance. I have to offload my demon cargo and get cleaned up. Then I need to sort out what's going on at Cloven Hoof. Merrie's in charge, so I know it will run smoothly, but I said I'd lend her a hand tonight. If I get time, I'll drop by and see how you're getting on."

Tilly nodded. "You might like to keep out of the way of that lot." She gestured to a guy in a cream linen suit with a microphone in his hand. A petite brunette ran along beside him, a harassed look on her face.

"Who are they?" They didn't look like the usual non-magicals who came to Willow Tree Falls.

"They're journalists," Tilly said. "They've been hassling everyone all day. They said they're here to get a feel for the place and do a piece to camera on the magic of Willow Tree Falls."

I grimaced. "That will only encourage more tourists." We had our limit when it came to non-magicals coming into Willow Tree Falls. We made exceptions on days like this, when the energy unwittingly drew them here, but I wanted nobody reporting on how fantastic this place was and turning it into the next hotspot destination.

"Look out. They're coming our way. I've already had to endure one round of questioning." Tilly hopped up from her seat and hurried away.

I wasn't so speedy and made the mistake of catching the eye of the guy in the linen suit.

He grinned at me, all perfect white teeth and dimples. He wasn't unattractive if you were into blond-haired, clean-cut guys.

He walked over, the hassled looking woman sticking to his side. "Do you mind if I ask you a few questions?" He looked at me and raised his eyebrows.

"You can ask. I might not answer."

His smile faded a touch. "It looks like you've had a hard day. Are you local to Willow Tree Falls?"

"Sometimes. How about you?"

"Sadly not, although it's a beautiful village. It's my first visit. Is there anywhere you can recommend for getting a true flavor of the place?"

"You could try the cemetery."

"Erm, I'd never have thought about that." His expression grew puzzled. "Do you work there? Is that why you're covered in grime? Hey, are you a grave digger?"

I looked down at the congealed demon goo on my shirt. I really should have changed by now. "Nope, I always look this good. Make sure to check out the thermal spas. Everyone says bathing in them brings a spring to your step."

"Perhaps you can show me?" Despite my grimy appearance, his curious gaze lingered on me for a second too long to be comfortable.

"I'm sure I'll be busy."

"I'm Nick Saunders. I'll be covering everything going on for the rest of the day. What do the mid-summer celebrations mean to you, Miss...?" He lifted the small microphone he held closer to my mouth.

I pushed it away. "It means the same as it always does. Too many people crowding the streets and eating all the cakes."

The woman beside him glanced up and grinned. "I've had far too many cookies. Your bakery is incredible. It's like the stuff is infused with magic. I just can't get enough."

I repressed a grin. She was closer to the truth than she realized. "Patti makes good cakes."

"I asked her for the recipe, but she said it was a secret. I've never tasted a cookie so soft and gooey."

"They are tasty," I said.

"If you're not interested in the solstice celebrations," Nick said, "what do you know about a mythical ring?"

The woman next to him rolled her eyes and shook her head. "Not that again."

This question interested me enough to respond. "Are we talking Lord of the Rings mythical?" I raised my eyebrows.

Nick nodded. "It could be."

"It's nonsense," the woman next to him said.

"No, Jenny, most legends stem from a factual basis. I'm sure there's something to this story. Think what a scoop it will be if we get the information before James."

Jenny shook her head again and shot me an apologetic look.

"I know nothing about a ring," I said. "I've read the Hobbit and the rest of the series. They're good if you're looking for rings of power."

"I prefer the movies," Nick said.

That didn't surprise me. "You can try Heaven's Door if you're looking for rings."

"Is that the store that sells all the pretty trinkets?" Jenny asked.

"That's right. My sister runs it. I don't think she'll know about a mythical ring. She's got nice silver stuff with stones." She'd even put a good luck charm on it if she liked a person. Aurora was always doing good wherever she went.

"No, I'm not into trinkets," Nick said. "I'm looking for—"

"There you are." A tall, skinny blonde woman wrapped an arm around Nick's shoulders and kissed him full on the lips. "I've been looking for you for ages. You told me you were going to get me a coffee. That was half an hour ago." She kissed him again and shot a suspicious look at me.

"Rachel, you know I have work to do." Nick shrugged out of the woman's arms. "I'm interviewing some locals."

"Oh, I thought this was going to be a fun adventure for us, not just boring work."

"It can be both," Nick said. His eyes tightened as he dodged another kiss. "Let me back up the stories on the hard drive then we can grab a quick bite to eat. Is there anywhere you'd recommend?" he asked me.

"It depends on what you like. Bite Me is lovely, but it's going to be fully booked on a day like today. Mystic Mushroom is good if you like pizza."

"Pizza would be great," Nick said.

"No, there are too many carbs in a pizza," Rachel said.

I rolled my eyes at the same time as Jenny, and she smiled at me.

"There's the Unicorn's Trough. Brogan does all sorts, but that's about it. There aren't that many options. It's a small place. Maybe you'd like to go to the next town." And not come back, I silently thought.

"Pizza will be perfect," Nick said as he glanced at Rachel. "You can always scrape off the toppings and eat them like you usually do."

Rachel wrinkled her nose. "If I have to."

Nick nodded, but his gaze was fixed on me. "You seem... different."

I straightened in my seat. "Different how?"

"It must be a trick of the light. Every time I look at you, I keep seeing a weird shimmer around you."

"Are you telling me you can see my aura?" I laughed and shook my head. "They aren't real."

"I must need my eyes tested," Nick said. "I could swear there's this sort of green mist around you." He sniffed loudly. "And a strange smell."

Jenny and Rachel sniffed and stared at him like he was talking crazy.

"I can't smell anything," Rachel said, her expression hardening as her gaze ran over me. It looked like she was assessing me for signs I might be a potential boyfriend stealer.

"Me neither," Jenny said.

"It must be your imagination," Rachel said. "Let's go get that coffee you promised me a million years ago. My feet hurt in these shoes, so I need to sit down."

I stared hard at Nick. If I didn't know better, I'd think he could see the demon I had trapped inside me. It couldn't be that. There was no way a non-magical would be able to see demons unless they wanted them to. I needed to get rid of Raksh.

"Are you sure you've never been here before?" I asked Nick.

"Absolutely. It's my first time in Willow Tree Falls."

"And it will be our last," Rachel said. "There's nothing to do around here."

"There'll be plenty to do later," Jenny said. "The village is just getting set up. Give it a chance. I hear they have an enormous bonfire over by those weird looking stones, and everyone dances around."

"It sounds positively primitive," Rachel said.

"Now, Rachel, you did say you'd behave yourself if you came with me," Nick said. "You promised me you'd let me work."

She pouted and blinked her false lashes at him. "I am trying, but I get bored so easily, and you keep ignoring me. What's a woman to do?"

"Get a life of her own," I muttered under my breath.

Jenny must have heard my comment because she ducked her head and hid a smile.

I looked back at Nick. "You have absolutely no connection to the village?"

"He's already told you no," Rachel snapped. "Let's get out of here."

"Hold on a second. I don't have a connection as such," Nick said as he pried Rachel's hand from his arm. "My great grandma lived here, though. In fact, she was something of a black sheep of the family. Everyone thought she was a witch."

I pressed my lips together. If that was true, it was more than possible that Nick had residual magic abilities he had no clue about. Sometimes, people did leave Willow Tree Falls. It could be that his parents moved away or their parents before them. If he was born outside of the village, he'd have no idea of his history.

"You should look into your family history," I said. "I'm sure your great grandma was a lovely woman. I hope she was treated kindly."

Nick shook his head. "She was taken away for some sort of treatment. I doubt it was kind treatment. Back then, it was routine to use electric shock therapy on people when they claimed they were witches."

"Come on, Nick," Rachel said. "I'm dying for a coffee, and your new friend looks like she needs to go change into something less grubby."

I looked down at my clothes and shrugged. I knew the mess I was in, but the cake had been too tempting.

"Everyone is heading to the stones," Jenny said as she watched the steady stream of people pass us, many of them with their faces painted.

I checked the time and nodded. "We move the celebrations there at five o'clock. People want to get there early to get a good spot."

"Why?" Rachel asked. "It seems like a hassle for such a small event."

I shrugged. "Beats me." I was done wasting my time explaining anything to her.

"We should go too, Nick. Maybe you can find some interesting people to interview there." Rachel gave me a pointed look.

Nick stared at me for another second before nodding. "That's a good idea. It's nice to meet you." He held out his hand to me. "I didn't catch your name."

I shook his hand. For a journalist, he was okay, although his taste in girlfriends was horrendous. "Tempest Crypt."

"Oh, you must be part of the family who looks after the cemetery. I talked to them earlier today. They seemed really busy."

Rachel laughed. "They sound as crazy as your great grandma if that's the case. How can you be busy in a cemetery? There's nothing to do. Everyone is dead. They're not going to be asking for snacks and foot rubs from beyond the grave."

I glowered at her. "You'd be surprised."

"There's always work in places like that," Jenny said swiftly. "Graves to keep tidy and lawns to mow. And there will always be bereaved relatives bringing flowers and little gifts that need tending. I think what your family does is admirable. It takes a special sort of person to care for the deceased."

I nodded in appreciation at Jenny's words. "They like it."

"Perhaps we'll catch up with you later," Nick said as he was dragged away by Rachel, who was glaring at me as if I was her new worst enemy.

"I shouldn't think so." I stood and walked toward Cloven Hoof.

Wiggles joined me after his unsuccessful pursuit of the other dog. "What was that all about?"

"Nosy journalists who need to keep out of our business." I glanced back to see Nick still looking at me. "It's weird. He could sense I'm carrying a demon."

Wiggles looked up at me. "He said that?"

"No, he had no clue what he was looking at, but he sensed it. He said he saw a fuzzy glow around me. That's Raksh trying to get out. Nick would only be able to see that if he had some latent magic ability."

"Huh, go figure. A non-magical coming to Willow Tree Falls, who actually has magic. Maybe he'll want to stay if he's digging the vibe."

"He's not welcome if he keeps that awful girlfriend with him," I said. "Speaking of girlfriends, who were you chasing?"

Wiggles' tongue lolled out. "She's not local, but she sure is cute. A pedigree cockerpoo. She's got the perfect fluffy cute butt. She could win awards."

"You asked her on a date?"

Wiggles grunted and nudged me with his nose. "She wouldn't talk. It looks like I'll have to find a female hellhound if I'm going to get serious action anytime soon."

"One hellhound around here is enough," I said. "Don't you go producing little hellhound puppies for me to deal with. I've got enough on my plate with you."

Wiggles barked out a laugh. "There's no chance of that. I'm a safety-first hellhound. And I'm far too young to be having puppies."

"You make sure the female who takes your eye knows that. No puppies allowed."

"My puppies sure would be cute, though, if an accident did happen."

I shook my head but had to agree with him. Wiggles' puppies would be adorable. Unfortunately, they'd also come with hellhound issues and would be unmanageable nightmares. Imagine toilet training a hellhound who farted brimstones.

"Come on. I have a demon to dump and a shower to take. Then we can go into full-on party mode."

Wiggles barked happily in agreement and trotted along beside me. So long as there was a party to be had and food to scoff, he'd be happy. We were very similar in that respect.

I looked forward to a fun night of amazing food and hanging out with friends.

Chapter 3

I loved the way the sun took forever to fade during summer. It was just dipping before the tree line as I headed down the stairs from my apartment above Cloven Hoof and entered the bar.

The warm amber glow of the recessed lights gave the red walls a friendly vibe. This was a place for magic users only. Non-magicals couldn't get through the barrier around the place. It was for their own safety. If any non-magical got hold of the produce I sold, bad things could happen to them. Magic was unpredictable when applied to non-magicals and needed to be used with caution.

I walked to the bar and grabbed a lemon drop from over the counter. Izzie and Brock were busy loading bottles onto the shelves at the back of the bar.

"Is everything going okay?" I asked.

Izzie turned and smiled at me, her face painted in sparkly purple glitter. "Everything is in order. We're ready for the crowds when the party gets going."

"Good. I'm helping Merrie outside. If there are any problems, just give us a shout." As tempted as I was to grab another lemon drop, I refrained. It had the same effect on me as a triple shot of espresso, but I needed to be balanced tonight, not frantic.

"Oh, before you go," Izzie said, "there were a couple of journalists sniffing around outside trying to get in."

"I hope you ignored them."

"One of them couldn't get in. He kept tugging on the door, but it remained shut as it should do."

"And the other?"

"That's the weird thing; he got in. It took him a few goes, but he stumbled through the door, and it slammed shut before the other journalist could follow. He walked right in here and started asking questions."

"His name wasn't Nick by any chance?"

"Yes, it was. Do you know him? I've never seen him around here before."

"You wouldn't. It's his first visit. Don't worry. I'll handle him. Just make sure you don't tell him anything about what we do here if he gets in again."

"No worries about that. I made out this was a regular bar, and we serve the usual beer and spirits. He had a quick half and then left."

"Good, let's keep it that way. He won't be a problem but let me know if he comes back again."

"Will do," Izzie said.

I stepped out of Cloven Hoof and inhaled the delicious smells in the air. I got a tangy whiff of barbecue, a sugary puff of cotton candy, and there was a definite scent of chocolate.

Wiggles nudged me with his nose. "We're going to have fun tonight."

"I hope so." My excitement faded as I spotted Nick hurrying toward me.

"Hey, I'm glad I found you," he said.

"I didn't know you were looking for me."

"You look nice." His appreciative gaze ran over my clean black pants and sparkly top. I rarely did sparkles but made an exception on nights like this. "I stopped by earlier, but you weren't about."

I raised my eyebrows and discreetly pressed a finger into the magic barrier around the building. It was intact. "Did you need something from me?"

"Everyone tells me Cloven Hoof is great."

"I've had no complaints."

He grinned. "Would you like to buy me a drink?"

I snorted a laugh. "Not any time soon."

His grin widened, his dimples popping. "I thought I'd ask. I don't want you to think I'm old-fashioned by offering to buy you one."

"Nobody is buying anybody any drinks." I went to step around him, but Nick moved into my path.

"There's something about you, something about this whole place that is different. There does seem to be something magical in the air. Is it just me, or are the colors brighter?"

"It's just you." I glanced at Wiggles and shrugged. There wasn't much I could do to help this guy. His family no longer had anything to do with Willow Tree

Falls. He most likely had a tiny bit of magic swirling through his veins but wouldn't be able to do anything with it. It was best he didn't know what really went on here. He'd only miss what he couldn't have.

Nick shook his head. "You're still glowing. I'd say it was a healthy glow, but it's still a little green."

"I need to get going," I said.

"I'll come with you," Nick said. "I want to do more interviews with residents. Hey, maybe you can be a future interviewee? Being a club owner, I bet you've got great stories to tell."

"That's not going to work."

Nick kept up with my fast pace, not seeming to pick up on the hints I was dropping that I wasn't interested in him keeping me company. "What's wrong with your dog's eyes?"

I slowed and stared at him. "Nothing. What do you see?"

Wiggles' eyes were now permanently red, the intensity of color growing when he grew agitated or angry.

"It looks like he's got pink eye," Nick said. "I've never seen it so intense before. Have you taken him to the vet?"

"He's not sick."

"It's contagious," Nick said. "Make sure he doesn't come into contact with any other dogs until he's better."

"Like I said, Wiggles is fine."

Wiggles pretended to act like a normal dog, sniffing the ground and cocking his leg up a nearby bush.

Nick watched him for a moment. "He looks healthy enough other than the pink eye."

"Tempest." Rhett Blackthorn appeared on the path as we turned the corner. He had his leather biker jacket over one shoulder. His dark, intense gaze shifted to Nick. "I'm not interrupting."

"No, Nick was leaving." I gave Nick a pointed look. "Don't you have people you need to interview?"

Nick's affable grin faded, and he glanced from me to Rhett. "Oh, sure, if you're busy."

I nodded. "See you around." I watched as Nick hurried away, glancing over his shoulder as he did so.

"That guy could not take a hint," Wiggles said. "And accusing me of having pink eye. I should have bitten him."

"He's persistent," I agreed.

"If he's causing you problems, I can have a word," Rhett said.

"It's nothing I can't handle. Do you need me for something?" I tried hard not to admire his toned biceps on display thanks to the white T-shirt he wore. We had history, but that was where our relationship needed to stay. Romantic distractions were not an option.

"Your guy is getting out of control. I thought you'd like to know."

"My guy?"

"Axel. He's drifting around the village telling all the non-magicals his father is a wealthy demon."

I groaned. "Someone must have sold him dodgy produce." My gaze cut to Rhett. "It's not your gang, is it? I've had to tell some of your guys to stop dealing in stuff they don't understand."

Rhett raised a hand and shook his head. "My boys know better than to do that. They don't want to cross you or your fearsome auntie. Josh is still talking about the time Queenie knocked him out and then forced him to ride pillion on the back of his own bike."

"That's right, and she'd do it again, so make sure they aren't selling anything they shouldn't. I'd better go see how bad Axel is." For the last couple of months, I'd been helping Axel Shadowsoul with his little magic mushroom misuse problem. He'd used them so many times that he'd gotten a taste for them and had trouble functioning if he didn't have a healthy supply of mushrooms flowing through his system. He'd twisted my arm and asked for my help in getting his head clear. We'd been spending a lot of time together, and quite often, it was time Axel used to try to worm his way into my affections.

"He was outside Sprinkles. I heard him say something about going to the stones."

"Thanks. I need to make sure he doesn't do anything he'll regret or that will get him noticed by the angels." My motive was selfish. If Angel Force thought the produce I sold at Cloven Hoof got people hooked, and it almost never did, they might take my license.

"It might be too late for that," Rhett said. "He's got issues."

"Haven't we all?"

Rhett fell into step with me as I hurried toward the busy main street. "I've got a couple of guys in the gang who had similar problems if you want me to lend a hand in getting him clean."

"We're getting there. It's just taking longer than I thought it would. It doesn't help when Axel gets his hands on supplies he shouldn't." I couldn't ask Rhett for help with Axel. They weren't exactly best buddies.

"Any time you need my input, just say. I had to come down hard on my guys before they straightened themselves out, but they're better men for it."

"If I need any muscle, I'll let you know." I indulged myself with a peek at Rhett's muscles before looking straight ahead and concentrating on not tripping over any of the non-magicals milling around. I had to remember I was just friends with Rhett. He was always there, offering his help and assistance. Most of the time, I never took him up on it. Now and again, it was nice to know he was there, watching my back, the same way he did for everybody else. Even though he liked to play the tough biker guy most of the time, there was a softer side to Rhett, the side that made my heart pound.

"Tempest, have you got a minute?" Dazielle poked her head out of Mystic Mushroom, a slice of pizza in one hand.

"I'll catch up with you later." Rhett nodded a quick greeting to Dazielle and hurried away. His gang operated on the wrong side of the law more often than not, and he had a tense relationship with Angel Force.

"You're hanging out with interesting company." Dazielle wiped cheese off her chin, still managing to look angel perfect, despite the grease on her hand. She wore her usual uniform of pristine white pants and a white shirt. Why did everything with angels have to be white? Surely, if they wore black like I did, they'd get more wear out of their outfits.

"Are you off duty today?" I nodded at the pizza.

"Not a chance, not with so many non-magicals around. We're struggling to handle all the lost children and drunken behavior." She took another bite of pizza. "A person has to eat, though. I wanted to offer you another out-of-town job if you want to go out again so soon. It's a nasty demon with a taste for virginal college students."

I laughed. "Good luck with finding many of those. What does he do when he finds one?"

Dazielle's nose wrinkled. "I'd tell you, but I want to enjoy my pizza."

"I can take the job. Give me a few days to straighten up things here, and I can head out again."

"This one's an Irish demon. I've no idea how he crossed the water, but he's causing havoc with the non-magicals. It won't be long before someone is killed."

"Send me the file, and I'll take a look." I patted my stomach. "While you're here, do you want to take this demon off my hands? Well, out of my gut?"

She stared at me. "You're carrying Frank and Raksh?"

"Yep, both on board and both unhappy about it. Raksh put up a fight, so I had to grab him while I could. He's kicking like a mule. I need him gone."

Dazielle stuffed down her pizza. She pulled a slim silver tube from her back pocket and flipped the lid. It was a demon canister and sucked those pesky demons right inside. "Cough him into this."

I grabbed the tube, turned my back so the non-magicals wouldn't notice, and coughed. Raksh shifted up my windpipe and stuck fast.

I gestured at my back. "Hit me," I wheezed.

Dazielle was never one to hold back. My ribs groaned as she slammed the flat of her hand onto my back several times.

I gave a huge belch, and Raksh zoomed out and into the tube. I flipped the lid shut and handed him to her. "One demon promptly coughed up."

"Good work." She tucked him in her pocket, slapped me on the back again, and waltzed away.

"Someone must have put a feather in her panties," Wiggles said. "I don't think I've ever seen Dazielle smile so much."

I grinned at him as I rubbed my sore back. "It's got more to do with tonight's celebrations than feathers being anywhere they shouldn't be. Tonight makes everyone happy. We all get a chance to recharge and celebrate."

"Including me," Wiggles said. "What are we waiting for? Let's head to the stones like everyone else and see what trouble we can get into."

I followed along behind Wiggles, soaking up the atmosphere and feeling a hundred times better now Raksh was no longer taking up residence. On solstice eve, Willow Tree Falls became even more alive with power and magic. Everyone felt good. I could feel my magic energy overflowing, and my fingers tingled with power desperate to be released.

A small side effect was that Frank was also stronger and had been misbehaving for the last hour, sneaking thoughts into my head and suggestions about letting him out for a quick play.

It wasn't happening, not this evening. No matter how strong Frank got, I was stronger. I was in control tonight.

As I reached the edge of the stone circle, the crowd thickened. Everyone, magical and non-magical, was drawn to stand inside the stones and soak up the vibrations. I walked slowly around the outside of the stones, touching each one in turn. There was something incredible about tonight, and I wasn't going to miss a second of it.

"Where have you been?" Aurora bounded up to me, carrying an enormous tub of popcorn. "You're missing all the fun."

"I had a bit of business to take care of. I'm here now. What have I missed?"

She grinned as she stuffed popcorn into her mouth, small pieces sticking to her glossed pink lips. "Auntie Queenie and Granny Dottie had a dance-off. It was hilarious. Everyone stood around them in a circle and clapped them on. I thought Auntie Queenie was going to pop a hip at one point; she was grinding against a stone and trying to twerk at the same time."

"That's something I'm glad I missed. Who won?"

"Granny Dottie, of course. She's so competitive." Aurora reached out a hand to me, her expression cautious. "Is everything good with you?"

She was asking about Frank in a roundabout way. We didn't often mention him by name. It only excited him when he became aware of Aurora. I nodded and grabbed her hand. "Let's take a look around."

Aurora beamed at me and skipped ahead, tugging me along behind her. I nodded at Merrie as I saw her at the Cloven Hoof stall. She smiled and waved me away. She looked like she was enjoying herself.

There were stands selling all kinds of treats, from popcorn to cookies. People danced around, even though no music played, and everyone we passed smiled and nodded, happy to be here.

As we walked around, I kept an eye out for Axel, but I couldn't see him. Hopefully, he'd decided to sleep off the effects of whatever he'd taken somewhere quiet and out of the way.

Despite the energetic vibe of the stones, I still felt a certain amount of bone weariness from my time away from Willow Tree Falls. Being away left me drained. Still, I wasn't passing up on the fun and was even convinced by Aurora to dance around the stones.

The next time I checked, three hours had passed. I couldn't have been dancing for that long! I leaned against a standing stone and stifled a yawn. All this partying was exhausting, and it had been a long day. I needed a time out.

I checked Wiggles was keeping himself out of mischief before creeping away into the quiet of the surrounding woods, making sure none of my family spotted me and dragged me back. I only had to walk for a short while before the noise faded and the peacefulness of the forest engulfed me. I trailed my fingers over a few of the trees, noticing how they vibrated with energy.

I sat on a soft pile of moss and leaned back against one of the trees. I needed five minutes with my eyes shut, and then I'd get back to the party. A quick nap to recharge and I'd be dancing again.

My eyes were growing heavy when I heard faint footsteps. I eased one eye open. It was the forest's wild woman. She rarely made an appearance and never in the daytime. I didn't consider her a threat. I knew little about her, only that she lived in the woods. She'd been here for as long as I could remember and thrived in the sanctity of the forest. She definitely had magic but kept her distance as she was doing so now, skirting around me, her cautious gaze fixed on my face as she slid past.

I relaxed against the tree and shut my eyes.

※※※※ ※※※※

A hand grabbed my shoulder and shook me. I gasped in a breath as my eyes flicked open. For a second, I had no idea where I was. In my confusion, Frank took advantage. His energy surged up my spine like a sticky dark mass, only becoming stronger when I saw it was Aurora who'd shaken me awake.

My hand went to her throat. "Are you crazy? Get away from me."

Aurora's eyes bulged as my fingers tightened around her neck. She blasted a spell into my stomach. It shot through me and made me lose my grip. I shoved her back and scrambled away.

Her eyes widened as she backed away. "I'm sorry. You were asleep. I didn't think Frank would be a problem."

Frank's energy curled up my neck. Once his hot power reached the top of my head, I was in trouble. "Get out of here."

"Tempest, I didn't mean it. I didn't know Frank would be in control when you woke." Aurora clung to the tree next to her as if it would protect her from the dangerous demon inside me who wanted her dead.

"He's not. Not yet." I held up a hand to block my view of Aurora. Even the scent of her was driving him mad. This demon was obsessed with my sister.

"I'm sorry. I'll go." Aurora turned and ran.

I gritted my teeth, focusing on Frank and shoving against his power. "Get back where you belong. She is not for you."

Frank purred with delight, but his energy sank an inch. "I'm just biding my time, little witch. That was a warning."

"Next time you try a trick like that, I'll move us out of Willow Tree Falls to some cold, magic sucking place demons hate. I'll stay there forever if you ever harm Aurora."

He growled inside my head and sank back further. "You wouldn't dare. It would hurt us both."

"It would be worth it to see you suffering." It would be awful to leave this place for good, but I'd do it. I'd leave if Frank ever became too much of a problem.

I noticed Aurora had slowed and hidden behind a tree, peeking out every few seconds, concern clear on her face.

I let out a shaky sigh. "It's okay. He's back where he belongs. What is it? Why did you wake me?"

She crept out from behind the tree. "I had to find you. Mom is upset. There's been a body found in the cemetery."

Chapter 4

I stared at Aurora. Had she taken leave of her senses? "A body in the cemetery. That's hardly news. That's where all the bodies go."

"Not a dead body. Well, yes, a dead body. Not one in a coffin and not one buried in the ground. This one was laid out dead for everyone to see."

I blinked slowly at her, my half-asleep, demon-muddled brain struggling to catch up. "Someone left a body in our cemetery?"

"Yes! Come on. Everybody is there. Angel Force is trampling over everything as usual. It's upsetting the demons, and they've made two new cracks in the last hour trying to get to the angels."

I shook my head. The last thing we needed was a bunch of angels running around the cemetery. It would take us weeks to calm the demons.

"Hurry! Mom is going crazy. She almost had a fight with Dazielle." Aurora gestured for me to speed things up.

"That I'd like to see." We raced out of the forest and passed the almost deserted stone circle.

I blinked in surprise. I must have been asleep a lot longer than five minutes if the party was over. Apart from a few passed-out non-magicals, everyone had gone.

We ran the short distance down the hill to the cemetery.

Sablo stood at the gates of the cemetery. She held up her hand as we approached and fluffed out her wings. "No one's to go in. It's a crime scene."

"We know. It's our cemetery," I said.

"Even so, I can't let you pass," Sablo said.

Wiggles ran out of the cemetery. "You're missing all the action. Where did you go? I was eating cake for half an hour tops, and you vanished."

Sablo took a step back, and her glare narrowed as she stared at my handsome hellhound. "He's not supposed to be in there."

Wiggles ducked around Sablo's legs and sped back into the cemetery. She spun on her heel and went to chase after him but then turned back to us. "He can go. No one else gets in."

Aurora grabbed my hand. "It's fine. We don't need to see what's going on in there."

"We do," I said. "Let us in."

Aurora gave a little shake of her head. "We can ask Mom later." She led me away from the gates and leaned closer. "We'll go in the side entrance. The

41

angels won't have a clue about all the ways into this place."

I grinned and nodded. Aurora was right. As guardians of the cemetery, everyone in the family knew the long-forgotten doorways. We hurried around the side of the cemetery, and Aurora tugged aside a swath of ivy, revealing a small wooden door. "Through there."

I yanked the door open, squeezed through, and popped out into the cemetery.

Aurora followed me, and we kept to the darkest shadows of early morning as we made our way through the gravestones.

"Who's dead?" I asked.

"I don't know him," Aurora said.

"He's not local?"

"No, but I've seen him around the last two days. He could be a non-magical."

I could already hear Mom and Granny Dottie's raised voices as they argued with the angels.

"We can take care of this business," Mom said.

"Not if there's been a murder committed in the cemetery. You might run the demon prison, but you don't control everything that goes on here." I recognized the sharp tone of Dazielle. She was not a happy angel.

We dashed around a large, gray stone crypt, and I saw everyone crowded together. Mom stood toe to toe with Dazielle, while Auntie Queenie faced off with a tall, blond male angel. Granny Dottie jabbed a finger in the chest of another angel, while Grandpa Lucius looked on with concern.

"Let's not deal with that right away," I whispered to Aurora. "Mom and the others can handle the angels if they overstep their sensibilities." We slid around the feud, passed the angels, and stopped by the body.

I stared down at him. "I know this guy! He introduced himself to me. He was a journalist poking around, trying to get a story on Willow Tree Falls."

Nick Saunders, the overly keen journalist who had tried to interview me, lay on the ground.

"What kind of story?" Aurora asked.

"At first, he wanted local comments on the party. He also mentioned a mythical ring. I told him that was rubbish. It's weird though. He does have a little magic running through his veins."

"He doesn't anymore." Mom came up behind us and gave me a hug. "I'm glad you're here. The angels are being obtuse. They're trying to stop us from guarding the prison. Can you imagine what all the demons are thinking having these angels trample all over the place?"

"Nothing I'd like to repeat in front of you," I said.

Dazielle strode over, her arms folded across her chest when she spotted me. "I should have known you'd be here."

"Always happy to offer my services to Angel Force."

She scowled at me. "You need to get your family in line. This is a crime scene."

I looked down at Nick's body again. "How did he die?"

"Someone hit him over the head with something heavy." Dazielle sighed dramatically. She knew she'd never get us to budge out of the cemetery. This was our territory.

The light wasn't great, but something was wrong with this scene. "Where's the blood?"

Dazielle's brilliant blue eyes narrowed. "That's what we'll find out if we can get on and do our jobs."

"I can't believe there's been a murder in our cemetery," Mom said.

"It's just terrible." Granny Dottie hurried over. "This is usually such a peaceful place."

"It is when you're not kicking demon butt," I said.

"That's to be expected," Granny Dottie said. "How are you, my dear? Did you have a fun solstice celebration?"

"It was great. It didn't end so well, though." I gestured to Nick's body.

"Definitely not for that poor young man," Granny Dottie said.

"I was telling Dazielle that we must help with the investigation," Mom said.

My eyebrows shot up. "Must we?"

Dazielle looked equally shocked at Mom's suggestion.

"Absolutely. This happened on our territory. We can't let that go unnoticed. If we do, before you know it, there will be dozens of bodies slung in here when people want to get rid of them. We don't want to be known as an easy touch."

"That's sort of the point of a cemetery," I muttered. "Dead bodies are supposed to come here."

Mom gave me a gentle clip on the head. "You know I don't mean that. This isn't a place we want people's rubbish dumped."

"Maybe Nick wouldn't like to be referred to as rubbish," Aurora said quietly.

"I'm sure he was a lovely non-magical," Mom said.

"He wasn't a non-magical," I said. "He had magic."

"He did?" Dazielle asked. "How would you know that?"

"When I was carrying that extra demon, Nick saw his shimmer sliding out. And Nick managed to get through the magic barrier at Cloven Hoof. Only someone with magic can do that."

"Unless your magic is weak," Dazielle said.

I glowered at her. "My magic is fine."

"If he has magic, who was his family?" Auntie Queenie asked as she strode over. "He doesn't look familiar."

"He doesn't live here. His family moved away some time ago."

"Maybe he was killed because of his magic," Mom said. "If that's the case, we must be involved in this."

"There's no need," Dazielle said. "I have Angel Force on it. We'll clear this up in no time without your help."

"There are thousands of non-magical tourists in Willow Tree Falls. Most of them will be waking up with sore heads in a few hours, and many will still be inebriated from last night," Mom said. "That's where your focus will be. You can't do everything."

Dazielle pursed her lips. "I'm sure we'll manage, but I appreciate your concern."

"I nominate Tempest," Mom said.

"To do what?" I asked.

"To help Dazielle. You did such a good job with uncovering who killed Deacon and clearing your sister's name. You should be involved in this, as well."

"No, really I shouldn't." I held up my hands as I backed away. Helping sort out the mess the angels had made when trying to solve Deacon Feathers' murder had been more than enough interaction with Angel Force. I'd only done it to help Aurora, not because I had a taste for solving murders.

"That's a great idea," Aurora said. "You were brilliant getting my name cleared. You must help this journalist. It sounds like you got on with him."

"I never said that," I said. "I put him off from poking his nose in where it didn't belong. He was trying to find some angle on Willow Tree Falls, and we don't need that. We have enough non-magicals coming here as it is. We don't need any more hunting for the one true ring or whatever it was that he sought."

"I insist," Mom said. "Dazielle, you'll have our full co-operation, providing you include Tempest in the investigation team. Do we have a deal?"

"I don't need to do a deal with you to complete this investigation," Dazielle said. She glanced at me and sighed. "But you weren't unhelpful when it came to Deacon's murder. Maybe you can lend us a hand."

I grimaced but saw the stern expression on Mom's face. She wouldn't want angels poking around the cemetery. At least, if I was involved, I could keep an eye on them and make sure they didn't do too much damage.

"Fine, I'll help." I wouldn't be here for long anyway. With the new demon hunting job Dazielle was lining up for me, I'd soon be leaving. I'd help out for a day or two and then be gone. I could manage forty-eight hours in the company of some angels.

An anguished cry rang out from the cemetery gates. Two women pushed past Sablo and ran over.

Sablo pursued them, her apologetic gaze on Dazielle. "They say they know the victim."

Dazielle shook her head. She walked over and stopped the women from getting too close.

As they neared, I recognized them. One was Rachel, Nick's clingy girlfriend, and the other was his assistant, Jenny.

"This is awful," Rachel sobbed as her tear-filled gaze remained on Nick. "Who would want to do this?"

Jenny stood awkwardly beside her and occasionally patted her arm. "It will be okay."

Rachel wheeled on Jenny. "How will this be okay? My fiancé is dead."

Jenny's expression grew puzzled. "I didn't know you were engaged."

"You don't know everything about our relationship, no matter how much you poke your nose in." Rachel glared at Jenny and then turned her tear-stained face toward Nick's body. "I must see him."

"Not now," Dazielle said. "We need to check Nick for any evidence."

"Evidence of what?"

"Foul play," Granny Dottie said.

"Foul play?" Rachel cried. "This wasn't an accident?"

"We can't be certain." Dazielle glared at Granny Dottie before turning back to Rachel. "Perhaps you'd like to join us at the station later. I can give you more information when we are certain of the facts."

"I can't leave him," Rachel said.

"Maybe we should," Jenny said. "We can't help, not now. Let's go get a coffee and give the police a chance to do their job."

"Don't tell me what to do." Rachel shoved Jenny away. She toppled over and hit the ground.

I strode over and helped Jenny back on her feet. We both watched as Rachel stalked away on her wobbly high heels.

"She's a charmer," I said to Jenny. "Are you okay?"

"I'm used to it." Jenny brushed mud off the back of her pants. "Rachel likes getting her own way. She always has a tantrum when things don't go the way she wants."

"You mean, she's a bitch," I said.

Jenny shrugged and nodded. "She has her moments. I need to cut her some slack, I guess, especially since Nick's dead." She glanced over to where Nick's body lay and looked away. "It doesn't look accidental to me."

"Most likely it wasn't. I don't suppose you saw what he was up to last night?"

"Not all night. He was in and out of the crowds, just like everybody else. I spent a bit of time with him but went back to the editing van and did some work. We've got so much footage from the celebrations, I knew it would take hours to cut together a decent reel for today's broadcast."

"When did you last see him?"

Jenny snitched her nose as she stared at the sky. "Just before midnight. My battery was getting low, and I needed to recharge my digital camera. Nick was interviewing a group of girls wearing unicorn horns, asking them about the significance of the horn. He was being really flirty. Rachel was nearby and was giving him daggers."

"Rachel's the jealous type?"

"Jealous and bitchy," Jenny said. "Not everyone's ideal combination."

"Did you see anyone else with Nick? Anyone acting strangely or being argumentative with him?"

Jenny twirled a finger into her dark hair. "No one like that. I did see someone strange in the trees nearby, though."

"What were they doing that was strange?"

"Their behavior wasn't odd, but they looked like someone from prehistoric times. It was a woman. She had long, dark hair and a crown of what looked like twigs on her head."

"Maybe she was a New Age type come to enjoy the celebrations." We got all kinds here, from upper class glampers with their designer, crystal-studded wellies and prosecco, to mud loving hippies with beaten up VW vans and composting toilets.

"Maybe. She didn't join the party. She looked sort of freaked out. She disappeared into the trees before I got a proper look at her."

My thoughts went to the wild woman I'd seen when I'd been in the forest. Maybe it was her, soaking up the party vibes like everyone else.

"You seemed surprised when Rachel mentioned she was engaged to Nick."

"Because she isn't, at least not that I know of. If anything, I think the opposite was about to happen. Nick wasn't keen on Rachel. She clung to him like a limpet. She rarely let him out of her sight."

"She's possessive as well as jealous." Rachel sounded more and more like a suspect if Nick had been murdered.

"I think she'd picked up on the fact Nick wanted to cut her out of his life. He was a good guy. At least, he was decent enough to me. I've only been on this job for six months and am learning the ropes. He'd taken me under his wing and given me a few pointers. There aren't many journalists who would do that. It's horribly cutthroat. If you're not the first with the exclusive story, then you're a loser. In this business, there is no reward for second place news stories."

"You liked him?"

Jenny blinked away tears as she nodded. "I did. As a boss, he was an okay guy. And I got to see a lot of his relationship with Rachel. He wasn't into her, not the same way she liked him."

"Why did he let her hang around with him if he wasn't interested?"

Jenny rolled her eyes. "Have you seen how long Rachel's legs are? And that cleavage she flaunts is not natural. Nick's a guy. He likes that sort of thing, I guess. I'm imagining he saw Rachel as a bit of fun, but she had other ideas. He couldn't shake her off, no matter how much he tried."

It looked like the decision as to who to question first in this case had been made for me. If anyone had a problem with Nick, it was his girlfriend. His bitchy, jealous, possessive girlfriend. Maybe he'd decided to break things off with her last night and she'd snapped. This mess in the family cemetery was the result.

Rachel would be the first person I'd query and convince her it was never a good idea to kill someone in a cemetery owned by my family. Not if she wanted to get away with it.

Chapter 5

After spending a few hours ensuring my family and the angels weren't going to come to blows and all threats of new cracks in the demon prison were under control, I left them to sort out the crime scene and headed out with Wiggles. After last night's festivities, I needed to check in on Cloven Hoof and see how the partying had gone down.

The sun was just rising as I walked through the door and breathed in the calm atmosphere. The building always had a calming effect on me. It was the main reason I'd leased it. When we weren't hosting pre-wedding parties or celebrating the solstice, this was a chilled-out place. It was a place people could come and relax and get rid of their worries. They could shut out the world for an hour or two, kick back, and just be in the moment.

It sounded disgustingly New Age, but it worked for me, and it worked for all my customers. Business was booming.

Merrie was behind the bar as I walked in. "I'm surprised to see you here so early."

"I grabbed a few hours of sleep after I shut the stall outside," Merrie said. "I wanted to make sure everything was intact after last night. It got wild for a few hours."

Merrie loved this place as much as I did, and I was glad for it. Whenever I had to go hunt a demon, I knew the place was in a safe pair of hands. "It all looks good."

"The place has been drunk almost dry," Merrie said. "I placed a rush order after I did a quick stock take. We've got enough to keep us going until that arrives. How was your night?"

"It started out well. Had a weird ending."

"Weird how?"

"Like a body turning up in the cemetery weird. And before you ask, not one we were expecting. This one was a journalist, the journalist who managed to sneak in here."

"No kidding," Merrie said. "Izzie told me about that. That is pretty weird."

"You're telling me. Now, he turns up dead in our cemetery. Mom's roped me into helping figure out what happened."

"Then you'll be needing these." Merrie grabbed a handful of dried mushrooms and tossed them into a small bag before passing it to me. "They'll keep you calm when you're having to deal with the angels."

I grinned. "Thanks, I think I'll need all the help I can get. If you're good here, I've got a bit of business to take care of."

"I've got no worries. Take as long as you need. I doubt we'll have many customers today."

I did a quick check of the place, changed my clothes, and headed back out. Wiggles trotted along beside me and kept nudging my leg.

"What's eating you?" I asked him.

"That's just it. We're not eating."

My stomach growled. He had a point. Breakfast wouldn't be such a bad thing. "What are you thinking?"

"Triple decker waffles. A few side orders of bacon. Pancakes and syrup. Maybe some muffins."

"What have you done to make you so hungry?"

"I was off enjoying myself while you were snoozing in the forest," Wiggles said. "This hellhound needs his energy after a night like that."

I glanced at him. "That didn't answer my question."

"Some things you don't need to know. All you need to know is I had a great time and burned off a lot of energy. Now, I need to refuel. So do you. I can hear your stomach rumbling from down here."

"Do you want sweet or savory?"

"I want both."

I grinned. "Let's go to Unicorn's Trough. Brogan does a great pancake stack."

"Now you're talking." Wiggles sped in front of me, his tail wagging as he led the way.

Brogan Costin was opening the doors as we arrived and smiled down at Wiggles. "What can I do for you?" He stood at six-foot-five and had a neatly trimmed beard he was extremely proud of. His muscled arms were covered in tattoos that stretched from his fingers all the way to the tips of his ears. If you saw him in a dark alleyway, you'd run the other way, but Brogan was as gentle as they came and loved nothing more than serving up delicious food for his customers. The only way Brogan would kill you was by overfeeding you all his delectable food.

"Hi, Tempest," he said. "Breakfast for two?"

"Absolutely, if you're open. Did you have fun yesterday?" I settled at one of the pristine wooden blue tables by the window.

"Yes, and despite having only had about two hours sleep, I feel wide-awake."

I nodded as I flexed my fingers. Although I'd missed the arrival of midnight, the most powerful time in the solstice, I also felt energized. I ordered two pancake stacks and enjoyed the strong coffee Brogan served as I waited for the food.

Several more customers came in all grinning and talking about last night's fun. It looked like the rumors of a body in the cemetery had yet to spread.

Brogan served up the food with a smile before hurrying off to wait on other customers.

"So, what do you think?" I asked Wiggles quietly, not wanting to draw attention to the fact I dined alone and talked to my dog.

"The pancakes are amazing."

"Not about the food. That's always good here. About Nick being found in our cemetery?"

"Oh, it was clearly murder."

"What makes you so sure?"

"You said it yourself, no blood. Someone must have tampered with the body. Anyone hit with something hard and heavy will sustain damage. That damage will cause leakage. Someone hid that leakage."

I grimaced. "Maybe he fell and knocked himself out."

"That still doesn't explain the lack of the red stuff on the ground. I had a sniff around while everyone was arguing. There was barely any blood in the cemetery."

I let out a sigh. "Maybe he'd had too much to drink. Nick could have hit his head on a gravestone and dragged himself along to try to get help. He collapsed before he could get any."

"Nope, someone hit that poor guy. It wasn't a death by being a drunken fool."

I rested my chin on my palm. "I think you're right." I pushed the last of my pancake around the plate, cutting it into smaller pieces with my fork as I did so. "Why did they have to leave him at the cemetery?"

"Beats me. I don't have the mind of a killer." Wiggles eyed my pancake. "Is that going spare?"

I tossed a piece to him before finishing the rest. "We need to check in with the grieving girlfriend. If what Jenny said is true, she doesn't sound stable."

"Rachel sounds like a nightmare." Wiggles' gaze shifted to the window. "Look, it's Aurora." He jumped to his feet and bounced on the pads of his paws.

Seeing Aurora reminded me I owed her an apology. I threw money on the table and hurried after her. "Hey! Wait up."

Aurora slowed and grinned at me but continued walking. "I can't stop. I'm late getting the store open. I had to break up two fights between Mom and the angels after you left the cemetery. She's not happy with them being there."

I jogged after Aurora until I reached her side. "I can't say I blame her. Angels make most people's skin crawl."

Aurora tilted her head. "They're okay. A bit self-satisfied at times, but then they're angels. I guess they're allowed to be."

We strode along in a companionable silence for a moment.

"Listen, I wanted to apologize about earlier."

Aurora jangled the store keys in her hand as we reached Heaven's Door. "What for?"

"Well, I strangled you. When I woke up, you startled me, and Frank reacted badly. I hope I didn't hurt you." My gaze went to her neck.

She shooed away my comment with a hand. "That's nothing. I blasted you with a spell. And I've seen you much more terrifying, even when Frank wasn't in control."

"Thanks a lot." I waited as she opened the door and flipped on the lights. The store came to life. There were rows of crystals, jars of potions, and herbal remedies. Books about magic, and charms hung from ancient tree branches Aurora had fashioned to display her wares.

Aurora did a great trade with locals and non-magical tourists who loved nothing more than spending an hour browsing the shelves and enjoying the friendly atmosphere the place exuded.

She flipped the store sign to open and turned to face me. "It was nothing. I should have been more careful. How are things with you?"

"No complaints."

"And how is he whom we never talk about? How did he like the solstice?"

"A bit too much. He's going to be a handful for a while."

"But he's being good now?" Aurora gestured at the space between us. "He doesn't have a problem with this?"

Frank often got antsy when I was around Aurora. "He's chilled out. How about you?"

"Oh, you know, same as always." Aurora glanced at me and wiggled her eyebrows. "I've noticed you've been spending a lot of time with Axel."

I shrugged as I leaned against the counter. "I'm sort of his sponsor. He's in magic detox."

Aurora smiled at me. "You must be getting close."

"Don't you start. We're friends. I'm helping him because he got himself in a mess. It's nothing more than that."

"He's not horrible looking," Aurora said. "And he's got tons of money. It must be lonely rattling around in that big old bachelor pad of his."

"I expect he manages," I said.

"Still, you're there now, so he won't feel so lonely."

"Like I said, we're friends. How's your love life? Are you still dating that old bloke?"

Aurora uncharacteristically scowled. "He's not that old, and yes, I am. Toby is being the perfect gentleman, as always."

"The perfect gentleman you still haven't told the rest of the family about." Aurora had gotten herself in trouble by hiding her relationship with Toby and had almost gotten charged with murder because she was worried what the family would think of her dating a much older warlock. A warlock who was being investigated by Angel Force for his dubious magic use and stealing from a wealthy woman.

"It's complicated," Aurora said. "We're taking things slowly. How about this for an idea? You take Axel home to dinner, and I'll bring Toby."

"How about neither of us does that?"

She laughed. "That works for me. You stick with helping solve this mystery in our cemetery, and I'll stay here and sell out of everything. No men allowed."

I watched as she hurried around the store, switching on the music and lighting up the jewelry displays. "I was thinking the girlfriend might be involved. I met her yesterday, and she was all over Nick like a cheap suit, demanding his attention, which he didn't want to give her."

"Is that the pretty blonde who shoved that other woman in the cemetery?"

"That's the one."

Aurora's nose wrinkled. "You're right to tackle her. She does seem like trouble."

"I'm going to find her today and see what she knows."

Aurora tapped a finger against her lips. "She came into the store yesterday."

"The girlfriend?"

"Yes, she looked around for a while and then came over and asked if I had something to calm her nerves. I asked the usual questions and made sure she wanted it for herself. I gave her two tinctures to try. She paid for them but then came back."

"What did she ask for?"

Aurora's eyes widened. "A love spell."

"She knows about magic?"

"I don't think so. At least, I didn't get any vibe from her that she has her own ability. She said she was having problems with a relationship and needed to make sure he was devoted only to her. I explained that love spells aren't all that easy, and you can't force someone to love you. She got a bit snappy and told me I didn't know what I was doing."

"Rachel sounds worried she was losing Nick," I said. "She came in here looking for a solution to her relationship problem. She wanted to trick Nick into falling for her."

"I suggested she talk to him rather than be-spell him. Well, of course, I didn't use the spell word, but I told her that my remedies don't work that way."

"I bet she loved that."

"She muttered something about me being a charlatan and stomped out."

"Then I definitely need to talk to Rachel. Did she mention where she was staying?"

"No, but she doesn't strike me as the sort of woman who'd be happy camping out in the fields or in a camper van. I bet she's got a place at Tabitha's hotel."

"Yes, good idea. I'll try there and see what she has to say."

Aurora arched an eyebrow, a doubtful look on her face. "I doubt she'll talk to you."

"I'll tell her this is Angel Force business. Just because I'm not carrying a badge doesn't mean I'm not assisting with their inquiries."

"Does Dazielle know about this?"

"She doesn't need to. She agreed I can be involved." I pushed away from the counter as the first customers came in. "I'll leave you to it. I'm heading to the hotel to find Rachel."

"Let me know how you get on," Aurora said.

"Will do." I headed out of Heaven's Door and walked to the end of the main street. Tabitha Dimples' hotel was a large converted house that had been separated into a dozen private rooms. It had a cozy, rustic feel to it and was always popular.

I entered the small, cream lobby with Wiggles and spotted Tabitha behind the desk, a pencil in one hand and her glasses perched on top of her head.

She looked up and smiled as she saw me. "What brings you here, Tempest?"

"Hopefully, one of your customers. I'm looking for a woman called Rachel. She might have come back here a while ago in a bit of a state."

"Oh, I know who you're talking about. Miss Fortesque." Tabitha sniffed loudly. "Ever since she arrived, she's been difficult."

"She's been causing problems?"

"Everything is wrong as far as she is concerned. The towels are too hard or too soft. The water is too hot or too cold. The bed is too hard or lumpy. I had to change her to three different rooms before she was happy. Imagine the chaos that caused at such a busy time."

"She sounds like a nightmare out of a fairy tale."

"She's been nothing but a pain in my rear-end since she checked in with her boyfriend. He, on the other hand, is sweetness itself. I've lost count of the number of times he apologized for that dreadful woman's behavior."

"He was the reason she was upset," I said.

"Has he gotten rid of her?" Tabitha's dark eyes gleamed. "I do hope so. That will teach the uppity madam a thing or two."

"It's something like that," I said. "They definitely won't be talking again. Any chance you can let me know which room she's in?"

"I shouldn't really." Her lips quirked. "Are you going to cause her a problem?"

"It's possible."

"In that case, how about I leave the book with the room information here and go make a cup of tea? I won't know one way or the other if you've had a glance and seen her room number." She tapped pointedly on a line in the book.

I smiled at her. "That will be perfect."

"Right, a cup of tea it is." Tabitha bustled away from the counter.

I turned the book around. "Room 108." I ran up the stairs with Wiggles and knocked on the door.

I waited a moment and heard shuffling on the other side. Rachel pulled open the door and stared blearily at me. "What do you want?"

"I'm here about Nick. Mind if I come in?" I pushed past her before she had a chance to respond.

"Who are you again?" Rachel followed me into the room. "You look vaguely familiar."

"I'm here on… Police business. I've got a few questions to ask you about Nick."

Rachel hiccupped and giggled. That was not the reaction I was expecting from a grieving girlfriend. "Oh, I figured someone would be by to question me. It's so sad what happened." She slumped on the unmade bed and picked up a small brown bag. She dug a hand in and pulled out a mushroom.

"Where did you get that?" My eyes widened. If I wasn't mistaken, she was eating produce from Cloven

Hoof. She shouldn't have been able to get her hands on that.

"They're these weird, sweet mushrooms. I know it sounds gross, but they're so addictive. Every time I feel sad or remember what I saw in the cemetery, I chew on one of these, and all my thoughts disappear. I get relaxed and happy."

"You bought them yesterday?"

"Nick had them. He left them on the nightstand." Rachel sighed. "Poor guy."

I held out my hand. I needed to be sure what she was using. My magic mushrooms could really mess with a non-magical. "Can I try one?"

She grasped the bag to her chest. "Get your own. These are mine."

Wiggles wandered around the side of the bed.

Rachel watched him. "He's very small for a Police dog."

"He's a puppy in training."

"Training for what?"

Wiggles broke wind loudly.

I suppressed a laugh. "Drugs squad. He's got a killer instinct for hunting all sorts of illegal things." I had to get those mushrooms. I couldn't let any other non-magicals get their sticky little fingers on my goods. "You must be sad about what happened to Nick."

"I am. He was my one true love. Well, he was someone I liked a lot."

"The police think his death might not be an accident."

Rachel cocked her head to the side. "I thought you said you were the police?"

"Of course, what I meant was my colleagues are concerned it wasn't an accident. Have you any idea who might have had a problem with Nick?"

"No! Nobody I know would do something so horrible." She ate another mushroom and smiled.

"How serious were you?"

"Very serious."

"Marriage and babies serious?"

Rachel nodded. "That's right."

That was not the story Jenny had been telling. "Did you live together?"

"Almost. I've moved most of my things into his apartment, but it's not official yet."

"Would you say you were both happy with the progress of your relationship?"

"Blissfully. I was always talking to Nick about weddings."

I checked her engagement ring finger, and it was bare. Their engagement must be a new event in their relationship if she wasn't wearing a ring. Rachel struck me as the kind of woman who would want a huge, diamond-encrusted ring to show off to everyone.

"Have you set a date for the wedding?"

"No, Nick was so fanatical with his work. Every time a story broke or he got a sniff of something dodgy going on, he'd shoot off and focus on that. He was obsessed. He was always promising me he was about to hit the big time with an exclusive story."

Rachel looked around the room, disdain on her face. "I can't imagine what he thought he would find in this little place. It's nothing but a tourist trap. Telling people those old grubby stones have magic in them, what nonsense."

I bit my tongue. Our beautiful standing stones were not grubby. "Was that why Nick was here? He thought he'd uncover some supernatural tale?"

"Something like that. He kept on about some stupid ring. The only ring I was interested in him locating was my engagement ring." She took another mushroom out of the bag and ate it. "I guess now that will never happen."

I glanced over at Wiggles to see him lying at the foot of the bed, chewing on a pair of lace panties. I sidled over and yanked them from his jaws. "Did Nick have any work rivals? Journalism is a competitive business."

Rachel sat up straight. "Now you mention it, if you're looking for someone who had it in for Nick, James is the person you need to speak to."

"Who's James?"

"James Ranger. He's always chasing after Nick and trying to steal his stories. You've probably seen him around here in the last couple of days. They've both been interviewing tourists."

I vaguely remembered seeing a tall dark-haired guy with a microphone in his hand sliming around people. "Would he have it in for Nick?"

"James treads over everybody to get what he wants. He was always coming to blows with Nick."

"When you say blows, do you mean physical fights?"

"No, more like verbal sparring. About a year ago, James stole an exclusive story right out from under Nick. He went to the source and bribed them to change a few details of the story. When Nick went to publish, he was blocked by his editor and told his story wasn't accurate. Then, James went and published the very next day in a rival publication."

"I imagine Nick wasn't happy about that."

"I should say. He smashed James's car headlights."

"So, they definitely weren't friends." This James needed looking into, but I still wasn't convinced about Rachel. She said the right words about being sad, but her actions suggested otherwise. "You won't mind me asking where you were last night?"

"I was doing the same as everybody else. I was at the celebrations. Everyone saw me there. I was with Nick most of the time."

"But you got separated?"

"Now and again. He kept heading off to interview people. I lost him just after midnight. It was when the fireworks went off and all those crazy looking sparks flew about everywhere. One minute he was by my side, and the next, he was gone. I looked around for him for ages. After a while, I got bored. My shoes pinched my feet, so I came back here, ate a few of these mushrooms, and fell asleep. The first I heard about it was when Jenny was knocking on my door telling me Nick's body had been discovered."

"You had no reason to believe Nick was unhappy in your relationship? If he kept walking off, maybe he was annoyed with you about something."

"Of course not. In fact, he's been thrilled this last month."

"Why is that?"

Rachel smiled smugly. "Because I'm having his baby."

I snatched the bag of mushrooms out of her hands. "Then you need to go easy on the sweet stuff. No more of these for you." Rachel was definitely not having any more mushrooms. I had no clue what my mushrooms did to growing babies. What if she gave birth to a baby who had magic, or horns, or the ability to fly?

Rachel pouted. "They taste so good. They can't be bad for the baby."

"You should stick to unprocessed foods. You don't want to give your baby a sweet tooth."

"Goodness, no. I definitely don't want a fat baby." Rachel patted her flat stomach.

"How long has Nick known about the baby?" I tucked the bag of mushrooms into my back pocket.

"Not long. We've been keeping it a secret until we're ready to tell everybody. He was a bit shocked when I first told him. It wasn't something we'd planned."

"He was happy?"

"Delighted. So, you see, I had nothing to do with what happened to Nick. I could never kill the father of my unborn child. I definitely don't want to be a single parent."

It was a convincing reason. I also couldn't imagine Rachel managing a kid on her own. Her lack of obvious grief troubled me, but it looked like she wasn't the only one I needed to speak to about Nick's murder.

I wasn't ruling out Rachel, but now I had another suspect. It would be worth speaking to James to see if I could figure out what he was prepared to do to get an exclusive on the solstice celebrations.

"You get some rest," I said to her. "There might be more police coming to speak to you in a little while."

"Haven't you gotten all the information you need? I need to take a nap and figure out what to do next. Nick drove me here, so I don't know how I'm getting home." She kicked her feet onto the bed.

"Call a cab to take you to the station."

Rachel's nose wrinkled. "I don't use public transport."

"Catch a ride in the big white van with all Nick's equipment."

"Don't be ridiculous. It's an equipment van, and it smells of old cheeseburgers and feet."

"I'm sure you'll figure it out." I gestured to Wiggles, and we left the room before I made any more ridiculous comments to solve Rachel's travel issues.

"That lady is as high as a kite," Wiggles said. "Did you keep those panties for me? I love lace."

"No, you disgusting dog, I did not. Keep your slobber off women's underwear."

"I don't know. First, it's no humping your pillows and then no chewing on underwear. How is a hellhound supposed to have any fun?"

"Chew on a bone and go hump someone's leg. Pillows and underwear are off-limits."

Wiggles grumbled under his breath as we headed down the stairs and to the front door.

I'd just stepped outside when I felt a shift in the air around me. I went to take a step and found I couldn't move.

"Hold it right there," Dazielle said. "We need to talk."

Chapter 6

The only thing I could move was my eyes. I swiveled them to glare at Dazielle as she walked toward me.

Wiggles jumped in front of me and growled.

Dazielle pointed a finger at him, and he froze to the spot.

"What are you doing interviewing our prime suspect?" Dazielle stood in front of me, her eyes sparking with annoyance. "I didn't ask you to do that."

If I could speak, I'd be uttering curses. Instead, all Dazielle's magic did was stir up trouble as Frank reared inside me, sensing the threat from an angel.

Dazielle snapped her fingers, and I found I could move my jaw. My limbs remained immobile. "I thought you wanted me involved."

"In a consulting role only. I don't want you talking to suspects."

"I can't sit around like you do, drinking coffee and eating doughnuts, while the prime suspect could be slipping away."

"We do neither of those things," Dazielle said. "But we do have to follow protocols."

"I don't. I don't work for you. If I want to interview people who are likely to have killed Nick, that's what I'm going to do." I blew out a breath as I felt Frank's energy curl around my spine. "And unless you want to meet Frank, remove this magic now."

"Cool your heels and get control of your demon." Dazielle narrowed the gap between us until we stood toe to toe.

"I'm trying, but there's an immensely irritating angel trapping me in her magic. Anybody would feel threatened by that."

"Let me take her," Frank whispered in my head. "Let down your defenses. I'd love to pound this angel into the ground. She is nothing but a problem for you. I'd be happy to remove that problem."

"Don't think I'm not tempted," I muttered to him.

Dazielle raised her eyebrows. "Are we going to have trouble?"

"We already have trouble. Drop your spell on me and release Wiggles."

Dazielle folded her arms across her chest. I noticed a bag in her right hand. "You need to calm down."

"And you need to stop being such an officious dork."

"This is a show of good faith." Dazielle clicked her fingers and pointed at Wiggles.

Wiggles growled at her. "You're treading on dangerous ground, lady. When I get free, I'm chewing on that leg."

Dazielle's eyes narrowed. "Open your mouth," she said to me.

"No way."

"Do it, or you'll be stuck in that spell all day."

"What are you going to do if I open my mouth?"

"Calm you down and deal with Frank. You might even enjoy it."

"I detect the scent of warm brownies," Wiggles said, his gaze on the bag in Dazielle's hand.

"I'm not going to do a single thing this idiotic—" Dazielle moved so fast she was just a blur. I found my mouth rammed full of something sweet and chocolatey.

"Eat that and relax." Dazielle pulled out her own brownie and ate a piece.

"Where's mine?" Wiggles asked.

"Chocolate is bad for dogs. You can have something else."

"What have you got in the bag?" Wiggles asked.

I glared down at him, my mouth too full to tell him off. He was so easily swayed by something sweet. Actually, so was I. The brownie was amazing. As I chewed the enormous lump of sticky, gooey deliciousness, I felt Frank's energy ebb and my mood improve.

Dazielle's anger also faded from her eyes. "I figured, since we are working together, I need a few tricks to get you to be more cooperative."

I finally swallowed the brownie and licked my lips. "And you thought that would work?"

"Hasn't it?"

My smile was grudging. "It helped a tiny bit."

"Good. There's more where that came from. How about I let you out of this freeze spell and we go to Sprinkles and figure out the next move together?"

"We definitely need to go to Sprinkles," Wiggles said. "I'm owed a cake. I got frozen as well."

"Fine, but I won't forget this," I said.

"I've no doubt about that." Dazielle snapped her fingers, and the magic broke around me. I noticed her tense as if worried I might strike back. She needn't have been concerned, the brownie had done its job, and I no longer wanted to kill her. "The coffee is on you."

"Fair enough."

We walked side by side along the lane and away from the hotel.

"So, what did Rachel have to tell you?" Dazielle asked.

"She did her best to play the role of grieving girlfriend, but I'm not sure she gives two hoots about what happened to Nick."

"What makes you say that?"

"The lack of tears and the fact she was laughing. She got her hands on some magic and was scarfing it down. Maybe that's what messed with her emotions. She reckons they were serious, though. Serious enough for her to be pregnant with his baby."

"Oh! I didn't know that. That changes things."

"Most likely. They could have had a falling out over the baby and Rachel lashed out, but she said she didn't fancy being a single parent."

Dazielle walked ahead of me and pushed open the door to Sprinkles. The place was busy, and we had to wait a few minutes before we got a table.

Patti rushed over to take our order. She raised her eyebrows when she saw us together but made no comment. "What will it be, ladies?"

"Two coffees and two blueberry muffins," Dazielle said.

"And a bowl of water and your healthiest muffin for Wiggles, who's eagerly waiting outside," I said.

Patti grinned and nodded at Wiggles through the glass. "Coming right up." She hurried away to the next table to take their order.

"I still think Rachel isn't off the hook," I said, "but she did point the finger at a rival journalist."

"James Ranger," Dazielle said. "I wondered about him. I saw him arguing with Nick yesterday when they both tried to interview the same person."

"The way Rachel described it, they were serious work rivals. They've got history. James stole a story from Nick. In revenge, Nick smashed up his car."

Dazielle nodded. "That would do it. Maybe with all the chaos of last night, James saw it as a good opportunity to get revenge. He lured Nick to the cemetery and knocked him over the head."

"Have you found the murder weapon?" I asked as Patti brought over our order and ran outside to give Wiggles his food.

"Nothing yet, but it looks like possibly a rock. There were fragments found in Nick's hair where he'd been hit."

I eyed Dazielle as I took a sip of my coffee. "You're being surprisingly open with this investigation. What gives?"

Dazielle chewed on a piece of muffin before speaking. "Honestly, we're crazy busy at Angel Force. With all the non-magicals here, plus out of towners with magic coming for the solstice, our workload has tripled. I've also had to send three of my team on a mission outside the barrier. I'm shorthanded, and we have too many open files on the desk."

"You're saying you actually need my help?" I grinned at her.

She scowled at me. "Your help would be appreciated, but only as long as you do things by the book."

"I don't read your kind of books, but I will get results."

"I can't have you charging in and demanding answers from just anybody," Dazielle said.

"I don't charge in anywhere, but I don't want to work in any kind of official capacity for Angel Force. I'm a freelance. I work best when I'm not stifled by rules."

"I agree." Dazielle ate more muffin. "Let's keep it freelance, same as always. That's how you operate when you leave Willow Tree Falls to demon hunt. I'll give you the information, and you feed back to me. I need to know what you're doing and what you have planned. Otherwise, it makes Angel Force look bad."

I grinned at her. "You don't need me to do that."

Dazielle's scowl intensified. "All I ask is that you tell me what you're up to. Give me the basics and let me know if you've got any new suspects. And tell me if you've discounted anybody and why. It will make our lives easier, and I'll stop blasting you with spells to keep you in line."

"It will take more than a few of your spells to do that."

"As I'm learning. Although, I see treats help. Maybe you're not so different from Wiggles."

I shook my head and glanced over at Wiggles, who was busy licking the crumbs off his plate.

"Actually, there is a suspect I'm interested in." Dazielle played with her spoon. "It's something of a delicate matter, so I wanted to give you a heads up."

"Delicate how?"

"Tempest, there you are." Granny Dottie hurried to our table, grabbed a spare seat, and sat down with us. "I've been looking everywhere for you."

"You have? What's up?"

She glanced at Dazielle and frowned. "We've been having a few problems with these angels. They're still not letting us have full access to the cemetery. We haven't been able to monitor some of the weak spots for several hours, and the demons sense a problem."

"Is there anything you can do about this?" I asked Dazielle. "You do not want a large crack developing and dozens of demons roaming around Willow Tree

Falls, especially since there are so many non-magicals about."

Dazielle nodded. "I'll head over to the cemetery. Everything we need should have been collected by now. If you tell my squad what areas you need access to, I'll make sure you get it."

"Well, that's decent of you." Granny Dottie sniffed, not looking impressed with Dazielle's offer. "It's not right that our cemetery has been invaded."

"It won't be for much longer," I said, glancing at Dazielle. "Will it?"

"We'll be out of there as soon as we can. We're trying to keep this as low-key as possible. We don't want to scare off the non-magicals or have a media frenzy descend on us."

Granny Dottie grabbed the remains of my muffin and ate it. "What are you two doing together, anyway? I didn't know you were best pals."

"In case you've forgotten, Mom twisted my arm to be involved in this." I gestured at Dazielle.

"Oh yes, of course she did. She always wants the best for Willow Tree Falls."

Dazielle cleared her throat. "Actually, you might both be interested in this. Someone in your family was seen talking to the deceased."

"So what?" I asked, not liking Dazielle's tone. "I spoke to him on the day he died. Do you consider me a suspect?"

Dazielle stared at me for a second too long. "No, but your Auntie Queenie was seen with him. Apparently, she made unpleasant threats."

"Are threats ever pleasant?" Granny Dottie asked innocently.

"No, of course not. What I mean is, I will speak to her to discover how she knew the victim. The fact she was heard making threats to him and then he turns up dead in your cemetery not long after is suspicious."

"You can't seriously think Auntie Queenie had anything to do with this." I shook my head in disbelief. Just when I thought the angels weren't acting like complete idiots, Dazielle goes and spoils it.

"The information source is reliable. And your Auntie Queenie used to run with the Dead Tree Witch gang in her younger days."

"About twenty years ago," I said. "She's not been a part of that gang for ages. And besides, being part of a biker gang doesn't always make you a criminal." It sort of did. Most of the guys in our local biker gang were on the shady side, but that was beside the point.

"I wanted to let you know out of courtesy that I would be asking her in for a formal interview," Dazielle said.

"Let me speak to her," I said. "I'll clear this up. Auntie Queenie sometimes speaks before she has a chance to think. She wouldn't have threatened anybody seriously. She didn't know Nick, so there's no reason for her to be involved with this."

"No, you're too close to this suspect. I will be interviewing Queenie. You need to stay well away."

"I don't think you should," Granny Dottie said. "We can't have Queenie thinking she's a suspect. It won't do her blood pressure any good."

"She is not a suspect. And you're not interviewing her," I said to Dazielle.

"I am. The source is reliable, and the threat she made was serious."

"Then check your source, because it's wrong." I looked at Granny Dottie. "It's time we left."

Granny Dottie stood. "Agreed. There's too much pompous angel stinking up this place."

Dazielle huffed and dotted muffin crumbs off her plate with a finger. "Don't you say a word about this to your auntie. I only told you because I want us to have a good working relationship."

"You can forget about any working relationship," I said. "You don't go accusing a member of my family of this crime. You're wrong. Stay away from her."

Dazielle brushed crumbs off her fingers and regarded me coolly. "I can't do that."

I shook my head at her. "Let's get out of here." I caught hold of Granny Dottie's elbow and hurried us out of Sprinkles before I said or did something I'd regret.

"Who does she think she is?" Granny Dottie glared over her shoulder at Dazielle. "Accusing someone in our family of murder."

"It won't be the first time," I said. "Those angels have it in for us."

Wiggles raced after us. "That was a stinking bran muffin."

"I thought you'd be full after chewing on all those panties. The fiber will do you good. Get things moving," I said.

"I do not enjoy lousy, tasteless bran muffins."

"It will keep you nice and regular," Granny Dottie said.

"I'm as regular as clockwork. Ten o'clock every morning, I head out, find a quiet spot, hunch down, and—"

"No! We don't need to hear about your daily bowel movements," I said.

"You brought it up, ordering me an inedible muffin," Wiggles said. "Anyway, where's the fire? Why run out on Dazielle?"

"The angels have Auntie Queenie on their suspect list for Nick's murder. Ouch!" Something squishy pinged off the back of my head. I spun on my heel and saw a squashed frosted angel cake on the ground. I looked back at Sprinkles. Dazielle stood outside with a handful of cakes and an angry glare in her eyes.

"Well, I never!" Granny Dottie dodged a flying cake. "The nerve of that angel."

Wiggles instantly pounced on the angel cake and scoffed it down.

Dazielle launched another two cakes in the air. One landed squarely on my forehead. The other Wiggles caught in an impressive acrobatic display as he leaped into the air and twisted to ensure the cake landed in his mouth.

I wiped frosting off my forehead before turning and stalking away. Dazielle had just sealed her fate. There was no way I would tell the angels anything I found out after this.

"That's more like it." Wiggles licked his chops. "Frosted angel cakes are the perfect tonic to bran muffins."

"Not when they're being slung at me as missiles."

"If you bend down, I'll get that frosting out of your hair," Wiggles said.

"We can't stand for that," Granny Dottie said. "You show those angels a thing or two."

"Don't worry. I will. One thing I know for sure, Auntie Queenie isn't going to be involved in this. I won't let the angels bother her."

I'd show everybody how incompetent Angel Force really was by solving this murder myself.

Chapter 7

I'd taken the previous evening off from figuring out who'd killed Nick and worked through my anger issues with the dumb angels. I'd taken a shift at Cloven Hoof behind the bar, done some paperwork, and then turned in for the night, still angry at Dazielle but no longer cursing her name.

I sat at the breakfast table in my apartment with Wiggles, enjoying a huge mug of tea as my thoughts returned to the body in the cemetery. "Okay, Wiggles, we have three suspects. The whining girlfriend, Rachel."

"Who is having the dead guy's baby," Wiggles said.

"That's right. The rival journalist, James."

"Who sounds like a scumbag and needs looking at."

"Agreed. And then, unfortunately, we have Auntie Queenie."

"Who can't be involved," Wiggles said.

"Of course she can't, but we need to give her a heads-up as to what's going on. There's no way she'd want to bump off a journalist. I can't imagine her threatening Nick. If he'd poked around the cemetery too much, she might have given him a friendly warning, but that would be it."

I needed to get Auntie Queenie out of the picture fast, so I could focus on the real suspects. I downed my tea, shoved on my boots, and headed over with Wiggles to Mom's for breakfast. I needed to find out how Auntie Queenie was implicated in this and stop Angel Force from hassling her.

Mom pulled open the door on my first knock, almost as if she'd been expecting me. She hugged me and ushered Wiggles and me into the kitchen. Glasses of green slime sat on the table. Granny Dottie, Grandpa Lucius, and Auntie Queenie all sat there, staring unhappily at the full glasses.

"Is this a new spell you're trying?" I stared at the sludge.

"No, I've got everyone on a health kick," Mom said. "We all overindulged at the solstice. I hear these green smoothies are a health elixir. You have one every day in place of your normal waffles or pancakes. It does wonders for the complexion and unclogs the arteries."

"It might do wonders for the complexion if you smear it on as a facemask," Auntie Queenie said glumly. "That is not going anywhere near my mouth."

"It tastes much better than it looks." Mom took a swig from her own glass. I saw her try hard not to grimace. "Maybe it needs a little something."

"Like tipping down the drain?" Granny Dottie thumped a fist on the table. "I want my usual pancakes."

"I'll add some banana next time," Mom said. "That will take the edge off the green taste."

"It will still taste like pond water," Granny Dottie said.

I settled at the table and waved away the offer of a glass of green sludge. Granny Dottie looked knowingly at me and inclined her head toward Auntie Queenie.

Mom sighed as she collected the glasses. "I don't know how any of you are still alive; you eat so many pancakes."

"Your pancakes are a health food," Granny Dottie said. "They give me something worth getting out of bed for every morning. If you serve me that green goo every day, I'll wither away and have no reason to live."

"Of course you won't wither away," Mom said. "Tempest, have you had breakfast yet?"

"Not yet. Pancakes would be great."

She shook her head as she pulled flour from the cupboard. "It looks like I'm outnumbered. Pancakes it is. But we will try green smoothies again."

"No we won't," Granny Dottie muttered.

I grinned at her. "Have you been contacted by Angel Force?" I asked Auntie Queenie.

"I've not seen any angels since they were at the cemetery yesterday," Auntie Queenie said. "They were a right pain in the behind. They cleared out late afternoon. I was glad to see the back of them, racing around pretending like they knew what they were doing and leaving bits of white feathers everywhere. It looks like someone had a pillow fight around the gravestones."

"They left thanks to Tempest," Granny Dottie said. "She put in a good word with her new boss."

"You're working at Angel Force?" Mom turned and stared at me. "I never figured you for that sort of job."

"I'm definitely not working there. You need to be an actual angel to work there. As you can see, I have no wings and do not fart angel dust."

"Well, you are working with them in an official capacity," Granny Dottie said. "Tempest has a lot of influence with the angels."

"I have no influence. I'm doing them a favor because they're running around not knowing how to handle their workload. Dazielle asked me to assist with Nick's murder."

"As I told you to do." Mom heated oil in a pan and whisked pancake batter.

"Yes, but we've hit a problem." I glanced at Auntie Queenie. There was no getting around this. I had to tell her she was a suspect. "Dazielle has a source, who suggests Auntie Queenie could be involved in Nick's murder."

Auntie Queenie's head shot up. "The very nerve of those angels. As if I'd do such a thing."

"I don't think for a second you did. But did you spend any time with the journalists yesterday?"

Auntie Queenie toyed with her fork. "Well, I did take the dead journalist and a couple of others around the cemetery. The demons were quiet, and I was at a loose end, so I showed them around and told them a few stories."

"What kind of stories?" I asked, noticing how Auntie Queenie didn't want to look me in the eye.

"Oh, you know, the usual sort of make believe that gets these journalists hot under the collar. None of the truth."

"Go on."

"I might have told them there were a few ghosts around, and if you turned up at a certain time of night, they'd see a ghost with glowing eyes." Auntie Queenie still refused to look at me.

"What else?"

"Oh, it's nothing. I was teasing them."

"What did you tease them about?"

"Just that there were rumors of creatures, who breathed fire, lurking around with long claws."

I groaned. "You told them there were demons in the cemetery."

"I didn't use the actual word demon. I simply described one type of demon we occasionally meet. They were fascinated. Although, there was one journalist, a snooty looking guy with lovely dark, wavy hair. He was cynical. He kept asking questions and trying to trip me up and make me look silly. I soon put him in his place."

"That must be James," I said. "I need to speak to him. He didn't believe you when you told them about ghosts and demons?"

"Not a bit of it. He kept making snide little comments and trying to be funny. But the other one, the dead one, he lapped it up. He was into it and knew a surprising amount about magic. He was very open-minded."

"How long did you spend with Nick yesterday?"

"He was there for a good couple of hours. He took lots of pictures and asked plenty of questions. He came by late afternoon."

"You didn't threaten him? Dazielle reckons someone overheard you making threats to Nick. They must have been the kind of threats that suggested you'd kill him."

"What's this?" Uncle Kenny stumbled through the back door, a strip of fresh willow bark in his hand and a huge basket of lavender over one arm. "Who's killing whom?"

"Oh, it's nothing, Kenny," Auntie Queenie said. "Someone's got their wires crossed."

"Queenie's in trouble with the angels," Mom said.

"Not again." Uncle Kenny wiped sweat from his brow, his dark brown eyes glinting with amusement. "Is this about you threatening to sacrifice those journalists to demons?" He laughed as he shook off his jacket and placed the willow bark in the sink.

My jaw dropped, and I glared at Auntie Queenie. "Say that again?"

"Well, I'm sure it was a joke." Uncle Kenny's grin faded as he looked around the room, realizing he'd put his foot in it. "I'm sure it was nothing."

"Sit down and spill everything you know," I said to him.

Uncle Kenny cleared his throat, and his gaze turned apologetic as he looked at Queenie. "It's just that, well, they were a bit full of themselves. Queenie thought it would be amusing to have fun with them. She meant nothing by it, but she did suggest letting out a demon who likes to sacrifice humans."

I dropped my head into my hands. "That's what Dazielle's source must have heard."

"Now, Kenny, that's not strictly true," Auntie Queenie said quickly. "The journalists were asking a lot of questions, and I got concerned they knew too much. And Nick was a lovely young man until he started asking about a mythical ring."

I raised my head from my hands. "I've heard mention of this before. What did he tell you about it?"

"Not a lot that was useful. He said he'd found a couple of letters that a great aunt kept. They had information about a ring that was supposed to hold great power. Whoever held the ring was able to influence other people."

"That sounds like mind control magic," Mom said as she flipped over the pancakes. "That's powerful. There aren't many people who can do that. Or control it."

"Is there any truth to this ring?" I asked Auntie Queenie.

"It's hard to say. There are stories of power being contained in certain objects. Certainly, things like crystals, stones, and metallic items can be infused with magic. It's possible Nick read about this ring, and it once existed."

"Not anymore?"

"All of those objects have been collected a long time ago. They're too dangerous and unpredictable to be in the hands of most people, whether they have magic or not. Our forest guardian looks after them."

I nodded. Willow Tree Falls forest was not just a place to take a lovely walk; it was a great place to conceal magic artifacts that caused more trouble than they were worth.

"Since Nick's got residual magic, could his family have been involved with the collection of this object? Perhaps a distant relative kept it, and that's what he's after."

"Remind me of his surname," Auntie Queenie said.

"Saunders. Was there a family who lived here with that name?"

"There have been a few," Auntie Queenie said. "He could be connected to the Saunders who used to live at the end of the lane."

"I shouldn't think so. They were gentle witches. They spent most of their time communing inside the stone circle. They'd have had no interest in getting their hands on such power." Mom dished out the pancakes and sat at the table to join us.

"I remember reading about a Saunders family who ran the Ancient Imp before Petra's family took over," Granny Dottie said.

"Yes, but again, they were your average hedge witches. They gained their powers from being surrounded by trees and plants, just like us," Mom said.

"Oh, if my memory is behaving itself, I know who Nick's family was," Granny Dottie spoke around a mouthful of pancake. "They were chased out of Willow Tree Falls."

"What got them chased out?" I asked. You had to do something serious to get evicted from the village.

Granny Dottie jabbed a piece of pancake with her fork. "I won't go into the details while we're eating, but it involves sacrifice. They would bring in non-magicals and use their blood to make the stone circle stronger. They believed the power of the stones could be enhanced and they could channel its energy into them."

Mom nodded. "That was long before my time, but I have heard stories about this family. They collected magic artifacts. Surely, all the items they'd collected have been destroyed."

"Maybe not all of them," I said.

"You're sure Nick had no idea he had magic?" Mom asked.

"He was clueless," I said. "When his family left, they must have started mixing with non-magicals and diluted their magic over the generations."

"It happens," Auntie Queenie said. "Some of those non-magicals are jolly cute."

I wrinkled my nose. I hadn't met a cute one yet. "Anyway, that could be the reason Nick was killed." The thought didn't sit well with me. If he'd been killed because of old ties to Willow Tree Falls, that potentially implicated everyone living here who knew the family. If someone figured out what Nick was looking for, they'd want to make sure he didn't get it.

"Can you imagine a non-magical having access to that much power?" Auntie Queenie's gaze turned worried.

"It wouldn't end well," Mom said. "It could destroy the non-magical. At the very least, send them mad."

"They wouldn't even know how to use it," Granny Dottie said. "Just having it in their possession would alter them, though. Items like that often have a malevolent influence. They subtly twist the owner to their will."

"If this ring is real, we need to find it," I said.

"And in doing so, you'll likely find the killer," Mom said. "If someone killed Nick for this ring, they could still be in possession of it."

"One thing I know for sure," Granny Dottie said. "We can discount Queenie from being involved in this. She'd never want to use such a magical item."

Auntie Queenie shifted in her seat. "I wouldn't mind giving it a go. It could be fun."

I raised my eyebrows and glared at her. "That almost sounds like a confession. You need to be careful what you say. Dazielle has you in her sights."

"Oh, she's all hot air and feathers. Dazielle can't seriously think I had anything to do with this."

"You're on her suspect list, but you're not on mine, so long as you're being truthful."

She shuffled around in her seat again and ate some pancake. "I am. I suggest you try that other journalist. He was too smooth for my liking. He was always eavesdropping on Nick's conversation and trying to get a new angle. He is not an honorable man. He even leered at my chest a couple of times."

"Don't worry. I'm speaking to him next. If he was tailing Nick that closely, he would have overheard him mentioning this ring or perhaps if he'd planned to meet someone who knew something about it. He could lead us straight to the killer."

"Be careful," Mom said. "He could also be the killer."

I studied Auntie Queenie carefully. She still wouldn't meet my gaze as she focused on her pancakes. What was she hiding? There was something she was keeping to herself about Nick. I was absolutely sure she hadn't killed him, but she was feeling guilty about something.

I could stay here and quiz her more, but all I'd get was the silent treatment, or I could go talk to other genuine suspects and see what I could shake free. I needed to get out there and start talking to people. Watching Auntie Queenie look shifty was getting me nowhere.

I hopped up from my seat once my plate was cleared. "Thanks for breakfast, Mom."

"Anytime. Where are you off to now?"

"To speak to that other journalist before he leaves Willow Tree Falls."

"Take care," she cautioned.

"Tempest can always blast him on his smooth butt if he causes her any trouble," Granny Dottie said.

I shook my head at her. "How do you know he has a smooth butt?"

She tutted. "Everything about that man is smooth. I bet he waxes. I bet there's not a hair on his body beneath those expensive shirts. And he smelt like he used a lot of talc. I bet he waxes and then stands in a cloud of baby talc to cool his sore bits."

I looked at Mom and grimaced. How was I going to get that image out of my head when speaking to James?

"Ignore her. I never know what she's talking about half the time." Mom glared at Granny Dottie. "I told you those pancakes are no good for you. You're on green smoothies for the rest of the week."

I hurried away as an argument started over green smoothies versus pancakes. I loved my family, but sometimes, I was tempted to let Frank loose on them. The things they argued about were never-ending. It came with a side order of love and affection and excellent food, but a witch has her limits.

Wiggles looked up at me as we crept out the front door before anyone noticed us leaving. "Is it time to sniff out a slimy journalist?"

"Yep, get your sniff on. Let's see what he knows about Nick's murder."

Chapter 8

I headed back to Tabitha's hotel to see if James was staying there. She confirmed he was a guest but had gone out early that morning and had not yet returned.

As I was heading back along the main street to see if I could spot James, Axel strolled out of Mystic Mushroom with a pizza box in his hand. I felt a little guilty. Rhett had warned me Axel was out of control last night, and in the mess of the murder and partying too hard, it had slipped my mind.

Axel grinned as he saw me. "How's it going?" he asked, his teeth gleaming against his perma-tan.

"Fine. Is that a late breakfast or an early lunch?"

"I guess you could call it brunch. I had a late one last night."

"You and everyone else in Willow Tree Falls." I arched an eyebrow at him. "I hear you did not behave yourself last night."

"Where did you hear such lies?" Axel's grin widened, although he looked sheepish.

"You got some of my produce?"

"Just a little. I promise it was a one-off, a treat because of the special occasion."

"It sounds like more than a little was used."

His shoulders slumped. "Sorry, Tempest. I let my hair down. I don't remember much."

"That's probably a good thing. Axel, you can't do this. It sets back your detox each time you do."

"I won't. Never again. I forgot myself. It won't happen again, not with you helping me." He lifted the box. "You can have a piece of pizza if you'd like."

I patted my stomach. I was way too full of Mom's amazing pancakes. "Another time."

"It's a date."

"No, not so much a date," I said. "I have been meaning to check in with you. I might not be around much over the next few days, so you need to take care of yourself for a little longer. Did you hear about the discovery of a body in our cemetery?"

Axel shook his head. "Nope, I only got to sleep just after dawn. Who died?"

"No one you know. A journalist called Nick Saunders. I guess you could say I'm working with the angels to help figure out what's going on."

"Tempest Crypt likes angels. Who'd have thought it?" Axel winked at me.

"Just don't let anybody else know, and the word *like* is not accurate. I tolerate them."

"I won't, so long as you don't point the finger at me like you did the last time you helped Angel Force."

I shrugged. "You were a good-looking suspect. I'd ruled out everybody else."

"You got the good-looking bit right." Axel jutted out his bottom lip. "I don't know how I'll manage without you. You're my rock."

Wiggles made an irritated sound in the back of his throat. "You should try. She can't babysit your sorry-looking behind forever."

Axel glanced down at Wiggles. "She's not exactly babysitting me. She's lending me a hand with my mushroom addiction issues."

Wiggles made a show of strutting away and raising his leg against the side of a nearby building.

"Don't mind him," I said. "He's not happy because he didn't get enough pancakes."

"I don't think he likes me," Axel said quietly.

He was right. Wiggles had never been keen on Axel, even before he could talk and voice his disparaging feelings about him. He thought Axel was far too smooth and confident and always sure he would get what he desired. Wiggles did have a point; as a trust fund baby, Axel was never short of admirers and had never had to work hard for anything if you discounted his recent failed attempt at becoming mayor. Still, I felt like I owed it to him to help him with his overly keen interest in the mushrooms I sold.

"I'll check in with you in a few days," I said to him. "Make sure you keep your nose clean while I'm distracted."

Axel saluted me. "You're the boss. And any time you want to share a pizza, let me know. I'm always happy to super-size my order so there's plenty to go around."

"I'll bear that in mind. I don't suppose you've seen any journalists around this morning? I need to speak to them about their dead colleague."

"I noticed people poking around the stones with a camera. They could be journalists getting some morning-after interviews."

"Thanks, I'll check it out."

"I can help if you like. I've got nothing on today." Axel's grin held a hint of hopefulness.

"No, you're good. You enjoy your pizza."

The sound of a rumbling motorbike engine filled the air. A few seconds later, Rhett idled by on his custom-built Harley. I couldn't help myself. My gaze shifted, and I watched as the bike drifted along the main street and turned the corner.

"If I got a bike, would you be more interested in me?" Axel's tone was light, but I noticed an intensity in his gaze.

"Bikes don't do it for me." I didn't want Axel getting the wrong idea about us. He was attractive, moneyed, and lived in a huge house, but he was not for me.

"Hmmm. I've noticed Rhett around Willow Tree Falls a lot more over the last two months. Are you the reason he's coming here more frequently?"

"I never see him. I've got nothing to do with that," I said. "Besides, I've got enough bad guy in my life with Frank. I don't need any more." As much as I tried to kid myself, Rhett looked magnificent in his leathers, sitting astride that powerful engine. I glanced at Axel. He had a good side too, despite what Wiggles thought of him. He'd proved to me he was more than an entitled trust fund boy. He had depth, but it was well-hidden behind his polished facade.

"Is Frank tempting you to plant a few more kisses on me?" Axel waggled his eyebrows. "I won't protest if he does."

"That won't happen again." I shook my head at the awkward memory of Frank lunging at Axel and having us lock lips. "I'd better head over to the stones before the journalists disappear."

I nodded goodbye, ignoring the look of dejection on Axel's face as I headed away with Wiggles.

"Do I smell a love triangle?" Wiggles asked.

I glanced over my shoulder at Axel. "You most likely smell the trash from last night."

"He's into you. You should take him for a ride."

I scowled at him. "What kind of ride should I take him on? Ferris wheel? Ghost train? Tiny steam engine?"

"Axel's got money. Think of the dog treats he'd buy me if you dated him. He's desperate for me to like him. I could get giant bones every day on the proviso I leave you two alone for fun times." Wiggles snapped his teeth together.

"You don't even like him. You'd hate it if Axel hung out at the apartment."

"But I love dog treats."

"I'm not dating someone because you'll get extra treats."

"That should be on your non-negotiable list. If your future husband does not provide your faithful hellhound with a daily treat ration, he must be instantly dumped."

"I'll bear that in mind when I revise my husband hunting criteria. But Axel will never be on that list. He's just in a mess, and I'm helping him out of it."

"What about Mr. Moody Biker? I smelt the change in pheromones when he zoomed by looking all powerful and intense."

"You cannot smell my pheromones."

"I smelt something. Undisguised lust, perhaps? Whatever, you need to get your love life sorted out."

"My love life is fine."

Wiggles made a point of looking all around, twisting his head to the sky, and then snuffling the ground.

I glared at him. "What are you doing?"

"Looking for this perfect love life of yours. I've not seen you get any action for a long time."

"And you're never going to." I groaned and slapped my forehead with the palm of my hand. "Will you stop discussing my love life? Focus on your own."

"Don't worry. I do. If I told you what I got up to last night, your ears would go pink."

"Then don't. Keep your horn dog antics under wraps." As we walked toward the standing stones, I had to admit my love life was non-existent. I was always concerned that bringing anybody into my life would cause problems, not just for me, but for them. The tricky thing was, when someone dated me, they also dated Frank. And I came with a talking hellhound with attitude. That was too much baggage for most people. Besides, my work kept me busy, and I was often away demon hunting. How would I find someone who'd put up with all of that?

"I smell ambition and cheap cologne," Wiggles said.

In front of us were a half-dozen people. I recognized the other journalist, James. He wore a pair of dark jeans, boots, and a white shirt. His dark hair was swept off his face, and he had a false smile on his lips as he spoke to someone.

He turned as I approached, said a few words to the person he was talking to, and walked toward me. "Do you mind if I get a few words?"

"Only if you share some with me."

James's smile turned puzzled. "Sure, I'm always happy to talk. It's part of my job, after all." He chuckled to himself.

"You used to work with Nick Saunders?"

James nodded slowly. "I did. I heard what happened. And you are…"

"Tempest Crypt. I'm helping with the investigation into what happened to Nick."

He held out a hand. "James Ranger. I'm a freelance journalist with the ITC. You've most likely seen me on the television."

"I can't say I have. I don't watch much television."

"Really? I always find it strange when people say they don't enjoy the television. You can live such an exciting life by watching other people act it out."

I suppressed a snort of laughter. "Yes, that's the reason I don't watch it. I like to live my life for real, not through a bunch of actors."

James shook his head, the look in his eyes suggesting I'd said something incredibly dumb. "Well, whatever. I guess it takes all sorts. What do you want to know about Nick?"

"How well did you know him?"

"We're in the same business, so our paths often crossed. ITC uses us as freelance reporters. He was a good guy but tended to jump the gun with a story."

"What do you mean by jump the gun?"

"Nick would often rush things through, rather than getting all the information. He had a tendency to miss the right angle, the real meat of the story."

"You were rivals?"

"We're all rivals in this business, but it was a friendly rivalry. I liked Nick. I never saw him as a real threat to my career." James brushed a speck of dirt off his sleeve. "I know the career path I'm on. I wasn't being shoved off it, especially not by a nobody like Nick."

James had just stepped over the line from confident to an arrogant moron. "Did you see Nick last night at the celebrations?"

"Of course. We were all there."

"When was the last time you saw him alive?"

James ran his hands through his hair. "It's hard to say. It was a crazy night. I was doing interviews and then edited several pieces to camera in the build-up to midnight. I can't remember seeing him after that."

"Are those pieces to camera time stamped?"

James's smile wavered. "Of course. You don't think I had anything to do with Nick's death, do you? Wasn't it an accident?"

"Most likely not. You did say you were rivals."

James rubbed his chin. "It was nothing serious. I even helped the guy now and again. He was out of work for six weeks on one occasion. I got him a freelance gig covering a local dog show. We looked out for each other, even if we did chase the same work sometimes. If you need to check my alibi, you can watch the broadcasts on the television this evening. I'll be all over it. You can see for yourself; I was standing by the stones just before midnight, filming the crowds and updating the audience on the exciting solstice fun."

"I might do that. How much longer are you staying in Willow Tree Falls?"

"Another day. But if Nick was killed, I'll stay a couple more days to cover the story. Do you really think he was murdered?" James rubbed his hands together, a gleam in his eyes.

"That's what I'm trying to find out." Wow, this guy was a total jerk. His friend was dead, and all he cared about was getting a story out of it.

"Can I interview you now? Get the inside scoop on the murder investigation?" James lifted his microphone.

"No, and you can't broadcast anything about it. Not until the ang—, I mean, the police have said it's okay."

"Aren't you the police?"

"I'm a freelance consultant."

"Oh, right. This is getting even better. A consultant usually means something juicy, not your average murder."

I shook my head. "Don't leave the village. I might have more questions for you."

"Not a problem. I'm going nowhere. I'm staying at the hotel if you need me," James said, "for anything."

I scowled at him, making it clear I was never going to be interested in anything like that. I turned to leave, looking around for Wiggles, who had loped off into the stone circle.

"Before you go, have you heard anything about this legend of a powerful ring in Willow Tree Falls?" James switched instantly into interview mode.

I feigned innocence as my heart sped up. "A ring?"

"It's something Nick mentioned. You see, that was his problem all over. He was hunting the wrong angle. We were here to report on the solstice, and he was hunting some ridiculous legend."

"If you think it's so ridiculous, why are you asking me about it?"

James's smile faltered. "Journalistic curiosity."

I knew I shouldn't, but I couldn't resist. James was a jerk, and jerks needed taking down a peg or two. "Now you mention it, there is a legend about a ring. Of course, it's not to be believed."

James's eyes lit up. "What does the legend say?"

I stepped closer and lowered my voice. "There used to be a family who hoarded magic items."

James arched an eyebrow. "Magic? As in witches and spells, that kind of thing?"

"Something like that. I expect, in reality, they were oddballs who didn't fit in, so people made up mean stories about them, a bit like you do."

"I always report the truth. People have a right to know." James scowled at me. "Go on. What about this family?"

"The legend goes that this family stumbled across something that had power in it. It could control people."

James licked his bottom lip. "What did they do with this power?"

He wasn't fooling me. He believed what I was saying. "No one knows. The family disappeared. Maybe the power consumed them."

His brow wrinkled. "Does anyone from the family still live here? They'd be great to interview."

"No, but before they vanished, they hid the ring in the marsh at the far edge of the forest." Most of our forest was lovely, but there was a small corner, the corner that dipped down before hitting the magic barrier, that was swampy and gross. Anyone who stumbled in there got covered in green, foul-smelling slime. It was the perfect place for James to spend the rest of his time and get the complete experience of Willow Tree Falls.

"The ring is there?" James's eyes gleamed with desire.

"If you believe the legend," I said, "which I'm sure a smart guy like you doesn't."

"Oh, sure. Hasn't anyone thought to go look for this ring? If it's not got any power, it could still be worth money."

I rubbed my head and made a show of thinking about his question. "There have been attempts over the years. But it's not true. Why would you spend time hunting for something that's a fairy tale?"

James pulled himself upright. "Of course, but my viewers love this sort of thing. They can't get enough of magic nonsense and go crazy for things like unicorns and fairies."

I shrugged. "I don't see the appeal."

"Hold on a second." James looked around. "Jenny, get over here."

I was surprised to see Nick's assistant hurry over, a harassed look on her face.

"We've got a lead on the ring legend," James said.

Jenny glanced at me. She had deep shadows under her eyes.

"You're working with James now?" I asked her.

"I guess so," she said glumly.

"Find me a map of Willow Tree Falls forest. Plot out the marshy area," James ordered.

"It's in the north east of the forest," I said, feeling a trace of sympathy for Jenny. I hadn't planned for her to go wading around in the marsh.

"How big is this marsh?" Jenny looked appalled.

"It's big. It'll take more than one of you to investigate it." I looked at James.

"She's not going to find this ring. I have to break the story," James said. "Jenny, map out the site and give me the details. Keep quiet about this. I don't want anybody else getting wind of what I'm doing. Also, find me a pair of wellingtons and some waders and a metal detector."

Wow! James was going all out in his hunt for a ring he didn't believe in.

"I'm on it." Jenny hurried away.

I watched her go. "It's good of you to help Jenny and keep her on the payroll."

"What else is she going to do? Jenny has next to no experience in journalism. She should be grateful for the chance to study a pro in action," James said. "She's a good girl and happy to take payment in kind if you know what I mean."

I wrinkled my nose, glad I'd told him about the marsh. I hoped he fell face-first in it and swallowed a couple of toads.

"Good luck with your search," I said brightly.

"Will do. Thanks for the tip," James said. "Oh, and as for Nick, I did see him with someone last night, someone he was getting friendly with."

"A woman?"

"Yes, I've seen her around a few times, so I think she lives here."

"Not his girlfriend?"

James shook his head and smirked. "If you can call Rachel that. Nick wasn't keen on her. I guess he figured he'd found a better option and decided to forget about Rachel."

"Who was the woman he was getting friendly with?"

"I didn't see much of her face, mainly because it was rammed against Nick's as they kissed. She was slim with blonde hair. She had a decent butt and an apron tied around her middle, like she was a chef or worked in a cafe."

My spine tingled as shock ran through me. He could be describing Tilly Machello. "Where were they kissing?"

"Inside the door of that restaurant. It's called something weird. What is it?" James tapped a finger against his chin.

"Do you mean Bite Me?" That was Tilly's restaurant. She couldn't have been kissing Nick, could she?

"That's the one. They must have had a romantic dinner before getting spicy for dessert. She's a fiery looking one, a lot better than that whining Rachel."

I stepped back, surprised by this revelation. Why would Tilly get involved with a non-magical? What had that kiss meant? It sounded like more than a friendly peck on the lips if James was being honest.

I went to say goodbye to James, but he was already walking away. I needed to speak to Tilly and see what she was playing at.

I called Wiggles over from his investigation of the stones, and we began our walk back to the center of the village.

He cocked his head as he peered up at me. "You look like you've seen a ghost. Did one of the spooks from the stones get you?"

"No, not a ghost, but I have had a shock." I still couldn't believe it. "We need to go to Bite Me."

"Is it lunchtime already?"

I checked the time. It was a little early, but I could eat something. "We need to find out what Tilly was doing kissing Nick the night he died."

"Whoa, that is serious. What's she doing locking lips with a non-magical?"

I had no clue. "That's what we're going to find out."

Chapter 9

I powered along the lane and through the door of Bite Me. The enticing smell of melted cheese and freshly baked bread hit me and made my stomach gurgle.

The restaurant still had its colored bunting strung across the usually more formal framed photos of scenes from around Willow Tree Falls, and the tables each had a vase of fresh flowers on them.

The tables were filling up with early lunchtime diners. I spotted Tilly behind the counter, bagging up takeout orders.

"You wait outside," I said to Wiggles.

He settled by the door. "So long as you feed me, I'll stand guard."

I grabbed a seat inside and gestured Tilly over to me.

She waved in acknowledgement and made a show of wiping the back of her hand on her forehead.

I could see it was busy, but she would have to make time. I was determined to find out what she was doing with Nick the night he died.

After waiting for about ten minutes and reading through the tasty sounding dishes on the menu five times, Tilly dashed over. "Sorry for the wait. It's crazy busy here, which I suppose I shouldn't complain about. What will it be?"

"Five minutes of your time," I said.

She laughed. "The chance would be a fine thing. I haven't had a break all morning. Heidi hasn't shown up. I guess she's sleeping off the after-effects of last night. I don't suppose you fancy waiting on tables for a while?"

"I will if we can chat first."

Tilly shook her head. "I'd love to, but I've got tables waiting and orders in the kitchen coming through all the time."

"I can wait."

Her expression became curious. "This sounds serious. Grab something to eat. Hopefully, it will get quieter in a bit, and we can talk."

I placed an order for two club sandwiches and watched with growing irritation as Tilly dashed around. There was no chance I'd be able to speak to her if customers kept coming in.

Frank stirred inside me, sensing my growing annoyance.

"You stay where you are," I muttered quietly to him. "I don't need you coming out and bothering Tilly." The last time Frank and Tilly had met, he'd destroyed her dessert counter and had me passing out in a tray of puddings.

That was one thing I could rely on when it came to Tilly; she knew how to handle Frank and was great at helping me get control of him.

His power curled around my spine in a sticky wave of evilness as he ignored my instructions to leave things alone.

"Cool your heels," I said, tamping down on my own irritation; it was only making him worse. "There's nothing to see here."

Tilly dashed over with the club sandwiches and dropped the plates. "You'll have to give Wiggles his."

I caught hold of her hand. "I have to talk to you about Nick."

Her cheeks flared with color. "Who do you mean?"

"You must have heard about what happened in our cemetery." I glanced around to make sure no one was listening.

"Of course. I don't know anything, though." She shook her hand out of my grasp. "Come and find me later. We can chat then if you like, but I won't be of any help to you."

"She's being disrespectful," Frank muttered, as I watched Tilly race away.

"She's just busy." At least, I hoped she was. I grabbed a plate and took it outside for Wiggles before returning to my seat.

"We could teach her a lesson," Frank said.

"School's out. No one needs to have a lesson today."

Frank had a bee in his bonnet about Tilly. The longer I sat there toying with my club sandwich and watching her work, the angrier he became. He must have been holding a grudge from the last time she'd knocked him down with her powers.

"We can leave if you're having trouble behaving yourself," I muttered to him.

"Not without teaching that witch a few lessons."

I twisted my head from side to side, trying to dislodge Frank's energy as it curled up the back of my neck. It surprised me how quickly he'd gained control. I was at full strength after the solstice, but so was Frank, and he must have decided now was a good time to test his boundaries.

I looked around the restaurant, busy with a mix of locals and non-magicals. It was a terrible time for Frank to make an appearance. When he did, he discarded all morals. Not that he had any good ones to begin with. He made me do whatever he wanted, whether that was gorging on desserts, destroying a restaurant, kissing a stranger, or ripping up somebody's clothes. And those were the things he did for fun. When he was in a bad mood, things took a much darker slant.

I stood to leave, abandoning my half-eaten club sandwich. Frank's energy slammed me back against the wall, and I sucked in a breath. Damn, he really was strong.

Tilly ran toward me, her mouth set in a thin line and her eyes wide. "Having trouble?"

I nodded, not able to speak. She grabbed my arm and yanked me through the restaurant and into the kitchen. "This way. I can't have you upsetting my diners."

"Thanks," I choked out, ignoring the curious stares from other diners as Frank's energy sent hot waves pounding through my body.

Tilly pulled open a door and shoved me through the doorway. Before I had a chance to realize where I was, she slammed the door behind me. I was enveloped in darkness.

"What is this?" Frank growled in my head.

"Tilly is saving me. I think she just shoved us in the freezer." I could see nothing. It was pitch black. The air swirled around me, kissing my skin with tiny, icy pecks. I imagined my breath shooting out of me like smoke.

"How dare that witch do this to us?"

"This is your fault," I muttered. "If you hadn't decided to get all macho in the restaurant, she'd have left us alone."

"She deserves to be punished."

"Tilly deserves nothing of the sort. You need to get over your problem with her."

"I need to destroy that witch."

I let out a long, slow breath. At least he was focused on Tilly and not Aurora for once. Tilly could handle herself, and after last night's solstice, she'd be super juiced with energy. Still, even I didn't appreciate being stuck in a freezer all because my demon was playing up.

I focused on controlling Frank, taking slow deep breaths, and trying to force his hot energy back down my spine. He shifted down a few vertebrae, inching back as his power slowly uncoiled from around me.

"That's it. Calm down. We don't need any trouble."

"We might not need it, but I desire it." Frank's energy surged up my spine, shooting up the back of my neck and covering my head. He had me. He was in control, and there was nothing I could do to stop him.

An unwelcome laugh slipped from my lips as Frank turned my body slowly around, my arms stretched out as he sensed the room we were in.

"Trapping a demon in a freezer. It seems like such a cruel punishment," he said. "Anyone would think Tilly doesn't like me."

"I'm certain she doesn't." I was conscious of my own thoughts but no longer in control of my actions. Whenever Frank took control, I felt like I was having an out-of-body experience.

"Let's see how much she likes me when I destroy her restaurant and maybe her along with it."

"No! Not Tilly." My heart raced as heat coursed through my arms and shot out of my fingers.

"Yes, Tilly. It's time this witch learned who is in charge." Frank pressed my hands against the side of the freezer. Ice melted down the wall, puddling at my feet.

I heard a thudding on the outside of the freezer. It sounded like scrabbling paws against metal. Wiggles

as the other was splayed, her magic continuing to pulse over me.

"Release me, witch." Frank's energy shifted, and I felt him losing control as the combination of magic and the pain from Wiggles' bite distracted him.

"Keep going," I managed to gasp.

Frank growled. "I need to have Aurora."

I sucked in air, nodded at Tilly, and forced my mouth open.

She shoved two whole strawberry tarts into my mouth so hard I almost choked. "Chew and swallow. These are Frank's favorite tarts. The sugar will take the edge off his rage."

I nodded as I gobbled down the treats. Frank was a sucker for the sweet stuff, and these tarts were just enough to loosen his control.

"More?" Tilly asked.

I nodded again. "Fill me up."

She stuffed in another tart. "You can let go, Wiggles."

He detached his teeth from my shoulder, and I hissed in pain. "Sorry. Tilly made me do it."

"I figured we needed a double whammy approach with Frank, pain and pleasure mixed."

I licked strawberry glaze from my lips as Frank's energy slid down my spine. "It worked."

Wiggles jumped off me and licked my cheek. "I didn't want to bite you."

"I know. I'm not mad." Although there wasn't a part of me that didn't hurt, it had been worth it to keep Aurora safe.

Tilly released me from her magic and held out a hand. "Let's get you up."

I grabbed her hand and stood slowly, suddenly conscious that we were being watched by a small crowd. "I'm fine. I just…" I didn't know what to say to cover up this mess.

"She fainted," Tilly said swiftly. "Happens to the best of us. The sugar from the tarts has her good as new."

I frowned. I did not want to be known as a fainter, but there were non-magicals watching, so I played along and pressed the back of my hand to my forehead.

We walked slowly back to Bite Me, Tilly keeping a tight hold on me, her magic simmering beneath the surface as a warning to Frank.

"I owe you one," I said.

"You owe me a lot more than one. How about you pay me back by waiting tables until Heidi shows up?"

I wrinkled my nose. It wasn't a terrible deal. "Okay, I can handle that."

As we reached the door to Bite Me, Frank's energy bucked up my spine. I shoved away from Tilly as he growled in my head.

"Knock me out," I said to Tilly as Frank creeped over my head. "Quickly!"

Tilly slammed me with a spell without hesitating, and I passed out.

Chapter 10

My head ached, and my throat felt parched as I blinked my eyes into focus. This was definitely not my bedroom.

"Take it easy." Tilly appeared next to the bed I was in.

I ran my hands down my face, my thoughts a muddled mess of strawberry tarts and dog bites. "What happened?"

"We knocked you on your butt." Wiggles' face appeared by the side of the bed.

I groaned. "I think I destroyed a freezer."

"It's toast," Tilly said. "Don't worry. The insurance will cover it. You seem to be making a habit of forcing me to knock you out."

"I'm trying not to. In my defense, you riled Frank up when you shoved me in the freezer. Maybe some warning next time?"

"And risk giving Frank the heads-up?" Tilly shook her head. "I thought the cold environment might calm him down."

Wiggles nudged me with his nose. "You were out of control. On demon overload."

"I know. It's been awhile since that has happened."

"Blame the solstice," Tilly said. "We're all hyped up with excess energy. It's just a shame Frank is as well."

I looked at her and shrugged. "I should be grateful you tried to give me frostbite."

"I'm happy to do it any time." Tilly smiled at me. "How do you feel?"

"Like I've been slammed to the ground, singed with fireballs, and bitten by a hellhound."

"Stop feeling sorry for yourself. I didn't bite you that hard," Wiggles said.

I tested my shoulder. There was only a small ache. "Have you seen Aurora? She really set Frank off. He got a glimpse of her, and that was it. There was no chance of me getting control."

"I have, but I sent her away. She saw what happened and wanted to stay with you until you woke up. I told her it wasn't the greatest of ideas in case Frank was lurking beneath the surface when you came to."

"Good thinking." I sighed and stared up at the ceiling. "I shouldn't have stayed after the solstice. But with a dead body in our cemetery and Auntie Queenie on Angel Force's radar as a suspect, I had to stick around."

"Auntie Queenie?" Tilly shook her head. "What's she got to do with this?"

"Not a thing, but you know what the angels are like when they get someone they're interested in."

"They're beautiful to look at but not the brightest in the village." Tilly stroked her fingers through Wiggles' fur a few times. "Listen, I know it's not my place to say, but you scared a few people today. Frank was strong. He could have caused real damage if he was in the wrong mood."

"I think your ruined freezer counts as real damage. And your chef dropped what looked like the most perfect chocolate cake in the world. That was a tragedy."

"I'm not talking about things. I mean people."

I frowned at her, feeling like I was being scolded. "That's your fault. You were the one who got all handsy and slung me in the freezer."

Tilly arched a brow. "Whatever I'd have done, Frank would have come through."

I looked around the room. Tilly was right, but I hated to admit I was struggling. "Things haven't been so easy with Frank recently. He's gotten control on more than one occasion."

"You can ask for help if you're having a tough time," Tilly said. "I don't mind lending a hand. Have you ever thought about yoga?"

I laughed and shook my head. "I don't think a downward facing dog will do me any good."

"You'd be surprised. I practise most days. It's very soothing. It helps to keep my energy aligned."

"I can show you some yoga positions." Wiggles did an elaborate stretch and balanced on his paws.

"I'm not getting into yoga." I looked at Tilly and shrugged. "I have been having a few control issues. I thought I could handle it. I figured I was spending too much time in Willow Tree Falls. Maybe a break away from the village won't be such a bad thing."

"If it helps you, then that's good," Tilly said, her tone suggesting otherwise. "But have you ever thought that you're running away from the real problem? By leaving Willow Tree Falls, you're only putting a temporary stop to Frank becoming a problem again."

"I can't run from a problem that's trapped inside me." I closed my eyes for a second. Tilly made a good point. Leaving Willow Tree Falls was the easy option when Frank became trying, but it never solved the real problem, how to dislodge one frustrating, stubborn, mean-spirited demon who lived inside me.

Tilly squeezed my hand. "One day, we'll beat that son of a demon."

"Here's hoping." I slowly sat up. "Enough about Frank, the reason I came here has nothing to do with me wanting to destroy your freezer or scare the non-magicals."

"That's good to know." Tilly grinned at me. "And it wasn't to eat my fabulous food?"

"Not this time." My expression grew serious. "Someone saw you locking lips with the journalist who was found dead in our cemetery."

Tilly's eyebrows shot up and her cheeks flushed red. "Who's spreading lies like that?"

"He wasn't here on the night of his death?"

Tilly nodded and ran her hands over the creases in the bed sheet. "He did come to dinner that night."

"And what else?"

"Nothing else. He ate dinner and left."

"He didn't stay for dessert?" I stared at Tilly as she continued to fuss with the bedding. "Not even your special kind of dessert?"

Tilly tutted and looked around the room. "Of course not. He was cute enough but not my type. I wasn't interested in him."

"Is that because you knew he had a girlfriend, and she wouldn't be impressed if she found out you locked lips with her man?"

"Nick was seeing someone?" Tilly pressed her lips together. "I didn't know that."

"Are you feeling bad because you led him astray with your amazing food and tempting ways?"

She glared at me and slapped the back of my hand. "I didn't lead Nick astray. Don't you go spreading rumors saying otherwise, or we will fall out. You'll have to find someone else to deal with that butthead of a demon when he gets too annoying."

Tilly never usually minded my teasing. I was onto something. "Since you didn't get romantic with Nick and had nothing to do with him winding up dead, you won't mind telling me what you were doing that night."

"Of course not. I have nothing to hide. We ran three sittings to accommodate everyone in Bite Me. As soon as the restaurant got quiet, I headed out and helped run the food stall at the celebrations. I was there all night. Hundreds of people will have seen me."

"You didn't disappear for a quick smooch break with Nick at any point?"

Tilly glared at me. "I should have left you face down in the dirt. I did not lock lips with Nick. And I'm not involved in what happened to him. It's terrible. Why would I want him dead?"

I raised a hand. Tilly was getting seriously out of sorts over this. "Did you talk to Nick when he came into the restaurant?"

"In a way."

"What does that mean?"

"Well, if you must know, he came to dinner and insulted my food."

"You're kidding. Why would he do that? Everybody loves your food."

"I know that! There you go. There's another reason I'd never kiss Nick. I would never kiss a man who doesn't love my cooking."

"There must have been something wrong with him if he didn't enjoy what you served."

"I was appalled. The worst thing was, he ate most of it before he complained."

"The guy must have been out of his mind," Wiggles said. "I always think I'm in heaven when I'm munching on one of your pies. And you make the best club sandwich."

"Thank you. I agree," Tilly said. "So, there you go. I wouldn't even have had him back in the restaurant, let alone stood close enough to kiss him after that insult."

This had me stumped. Tilly was fiercely passionate about the food she served. Everything was fresh and locally produced. I'd never had a bad meal at Bite Me, and I was absolutely sure that, if anyone insulted her cooking, she'd sling them out the door.

"Maybe it was somebody else seen kissing Nick." I eased myself off the bed.

Tilly held out a hand in case I needed it as I stood. "It must have been because it wasn't me."

I straightened my clothes and smoothed a hand over my hair. "Thanks for saving me from Frank. Let me know if you have any problems with getting a pay-out for your freezer. I don't want to see you out of pocket for what happened."

Tilly waved a hand at me in a dismissive gesture. "Don't worry about it. I'll get it sorted. Do you feel safe to leave?"

"Frank is not stirring. You well and truly whipped him this time."

"It was close." Tilly led the way down the stairs and back into the restaurant. "If I hadn't had Wiggles helping me, I'd have struggled."

"Just call me Iron Fist the Wonder Dog," Wiggles said.

"Iron Fist?"

"Don't pay him any attention. Wiggles has been trying to change his name ever since he got his voice."

Tilly grinned, petted his head, and gave Wiggles a muffin. "This is your reward, Iron Fist."

Wiggles grabbed the muffin and trotted out of the restaurant ahead of me.

I said goodbye to Tilly and walked out onto the main street. I felt none the wiser for my conversation with her, but she'd acted shifty when I'd quizzed her about kissing Nick. Maybe James had been mistaken, and he hadn't seen Nick with her but another mysterious blonde wearing an apron.

I walked slowly back to Cloven Hoof with Wiggles. I had to figure out my next move to find out who killed Nick. But first, I needed to clean myself up and wash off the unpleasant tang of demon and dirt.

Chapter 11

As I shoved open the door to Cloven Hoof, the unwelcome scent of warm, downy feathers hit me. Dazielle sat at the bar, a half-empty glass in front of her.

She turned in her seat and nodded at me. "I figured we needed to talk."

I glowered at her, my fingers automatically clenching. "Have you got any more cakes you're intending to throw at me?"

Dazielle smirked. "I couldn't help myself. You and your granny stomped off like a pair of big kids."

"And you acted just as maturely by hurling cake?"

"I decided to sink to your level. It was a terrible waste of cake, but it was worth it to see the look on your faces." Dazielle's smirk grew. "You have to admit you overreacted when I suggested your aunt was involved in Nick Saunders' murder."

"You'd have done the same if I'd accused a member of your family of murder." I strode over and sat on the stool next to her.

"Maybe, maybe not. I like to think I will always be on the right side of justice, no matter who committed the crime."

I wrinkled my nose. I would need to deep clean this place if Dazielle got any smugger.

Dazielle looked away, and some of her smugness faded. "I wanted to be open with you about what we've found. I trust you'll do the same."

"I'll consider it."

She arched an eyebrow. "Have you had a chance to speak to your aunt and figure out what she was doing?"

I twisted my mouth to the side. That was the annoying thing. I had, and Auntie Queenie had been less than forthcoming. She'd hidden the fact she'd made threats to Nick, even if it had been in jest. If it hadn't been for Uncle Kenny blundering in and revealing the truth, she most likely wouldn't have said a thing about it.

"Your silence suggests all is not well."

"Fine, Auntie Queenie acted a bit shady when I spoke to her. But she didn't mean anything by what she said to Nick."

"Which was?"

"She said something about summoning a demon who sacrifices humans."

Dazielle coughed on the sip of drink she'd just taken. "She was joking?"

"She only ever jokes about things like that. And she only summons demons when she absolutely has to do so."

"I'll pretend I didn't hear that."

"Good, because that was a joke too. You see, people make dumb jokes all the time. Anyway, whatever she's concealing, it's nothing serious. I've also spoken to James Ranger, the other journalist."

"What were your impressions of him?"

I smiled to myself as I pictured James sliding about in the marsh. I hoped he was having fun. "James claims any rivalry he had with Nick was friendly, which doesn't tally with what Rachel told me."

The main door to Cloven Hoof opened. My eyebrows shot up when I saw Jenny, Nick's former assistant, come in. How was she here? She shouldn't be able to get through the magic barrier that prevented non-magicals getting access.

Maybe my magic was on the blink. First Nick and now Jenny had broken through it. It should be impossible. When I got a moment, I'd strengthen the barrier and make sure no more non-magicals stumbled in and saw anything they shouldn't.

Jenny waved when she saw me and hurried over. "I hope I'm not intruding." She glanced at Dazielle and nodded.

"No, what do you need?"

Jenny puffed out a breath. "This is going to sound silly, and I apologize in advance for asking, but James insisted I come by and speak to you."

"About what?"

Jenny tugged at the end of her hair and shuffled her feet. "I'm almost too embarrassed to say. It's just that James has had a few people report that they saw you being chased by the woman from the restaurant and your dog."

I glanced at Dazielle, who looked at me with a curious expression on her face. It looked like she'd missed that bit of news. "What if I was?"

Jenny's eyes widened. "Oh, I didn't expect you to say that. Well, that's not so strange, I guess, but the weird thing is, people also reported seeing smoke coming out of your mouth."

I ignored the hard glare Dazielle gave me. It seemed some other non-magicals attending the solstice celebrations also had a hidden magic radar. Rather than seeing me being chased by a dog and my friend, they'd seen Frank's energy spiraling out of me. Note to future self: do not let Frank get control when Willow Tree Falls is full of non-magicals.

Jenny gave an embarrassed sounding laugh when I didn't reply. "Oh, goodness, I really am sorry about this. I knew James was setting me up. He loves humiliating people. It must be a joke. Of course, that's what it is."

"It sounds like it must be. I think it's impossible for people to breathe smoke." I leaned toward her. "And I'm not a half-dragon in disguise."

Jenny grinned. "I expect he'll ask me to go buy a long wait next. He thinks I'm an idiot. I just proved him right."

"You're not an idiot. When he's not wasting your time, how are you getting on being James's assistant?"

Jenny's smile faded. "Well, it's a job, of sorts. I don't think he's planning on paying me, not like Nick was. I keep trying to get him to confirm my wages, but he gets all evasive. What else can I do? I came here with Nick as a part of his team, and we need to finish the story. I'll have to look for someone else to apprentice with when this is over."

"You're not planning on sticking with James when you get out of here?"

"Good grief, not for a second." Jenny's expression turned startled. "I mean, he's okay, but he doesn't need an assistant. I'm sure he works better alone."

I could imagine James had enough ego for several people not to need it bolstered by Jenny. "How's everything going with your work?"

"It's all a bit messy. I have some work I did for Nick waiting to be edited. Then there's stuff from James that he's insisting I focus on. I feel like I'm being torn in two different directions."

"You must miss Nick. It sounds like he treated you a lot better than James."

"He was a good guy to work for. I hope you figure out what happened to him quickly. James keeps on about getting an exclusive on the story. I feel sick about reporting on the death of a friend."

"No doubt. We're working on it," I said. "We're following several leads."

"If there's anything I can do, let me know." Jenny looked around the bar. "I'd better go, or James will only complain about me. Again, I'm so sorry for asking you those stupid questions about the smoke."

"No problem. Maybe you need to take what James tells you with a pinch of salt, so he doesn't have you running all over the village wasting your time."

"You're absolutely right." She waved a quick goodbye and hurried away.

I needed to follow my own advice when it came to time wasters. James had pointed the finger at Tilly and suggested a romantic involvement between her and Nick. He could be distracting me from his own motives for wanting Nick dead.

"What do you think of her?" Dazielle asked as Jenny left the bar.

"I don't think Jenny's involved. I asked her where she was the night Nick died. She's got a good alibi. She also seems a bit too—"

"Too timid? Too innocent?"

"Both. She's not got a mean streak in her like Rachel. Somebody must have seen what happened to Nick that night. There were so many people around. How do you kill someone at such a busy event and it goes unnoticed?"

"There wouldn't have been anyone in your cemetery."

"There'd have been members of my family," I said. "Before you start accusing my aunt again, it wasn't her. Besides, we always know when we get people blundering into the cemetery and nosing around. We discourage it, but somehow, they still sneak in. We'd have known if someone had been murdered there."

"You weren't in the cemetery with anyone that night?"

"I don't often do cemetery duty. I was in the forest, getting some shuteye. The first thing I knew about the murder was when Aurora woke me and told me what had happened." I tapped my fingers on the top of the bar. "I did see someone else in the forest. It was the wild woman, the lady with the long dreadlocked hair."

"You're talking about Jane Doe?"

"Erm, I don't know her name."

Dazielle arched a brow. "Exactly."

"Oh, got it. Anyway, Jane might have seen what happened. She's good at sneaking around and nobody seeing her."

"Only seeing something? Could she have had something to do with Nick's murder?"

"There'd be no reason she would be involved. I'll ask her. If nothing else, Jane might have seen someone lurking around or following Nick and waiting for the opportunity to attack."

"Good luck with finding her. Jane does not get found easily. She finds you, not the other way around."

I shrugged. "That won't be a problem." The chances were Jane, or whatever her real name was, kept out of the angels' way deliberately.

Dazielle stood. "A word of advice. From what I've just heard, you need to keep better control of Frank."

"I control him just fine." I grabbed a drink stirrer and swirled it around my fingers.

"Not from Jenny's account of what happened to you."

"She was exaggerating. I was out for a jog, not being chased."

Dazielle snorted a most un-angel-like laugh. "You do not jog."

"Maybe I just took it up."

Dazielle tutted. "If you're having problems, I need to know. I can't have you becoming a threat to other residents or the non-magicals."

"We can't scare off the non-magicals. That would be too sad."

"Mannie has plans for Willow Tree Falls. That means we're to be more accommodating to the growing numbers of non-magicals. They do not like demons."

My nose wrinkled. Mannie Winter, our new mayor, was determined to double non-magical tourist numbers. "Then they should hate this place, given what my family does."

"You don't want a non-magical to uncover your secret. I can't imagine you'd ever want to be front page news. What would the headlines be: I Swallow Demons for Breakfast. My Best Friend's a Demon. Or how about—"

"Enough! As if they'd believe I carry a demon inside of me."

Dazielle shrugged. "You've heard of voodoo? People have died having their demons exorcised."

I waved her away. Her comments were nonsense. Frank was strong, but I was stronger, and he wasn't catching me out again. "I'll find you later when I have something new about the case."

Dazielle gave me a shrewd look before nodding. "Suit yourself." She strode away, a cascade of tiny white feathers floating off her.

I watched her go, trying to ignore the urge to lob something at her head. We had a truce, but it felt like a temporary one. The sooner I figured out who killed Nick Saunders, the sooner I could get the angels off my back and out of my bar.

Chapter 12

After spending a long afternoon sorting admin at Cloven Hoof, I headed out with Wiggles to see if I could find Jane in the forest. There was no point in going until late; she never came out until dark. At least, I'd never seen her strolling through Willow Tree Falls in the middle of the day. Our wild woman of the forest lived the life of a card-carrying hermit.

I stopped at Sprinkles just before Patti closed and grabbed a fresh out of the oven apple pie covered with cinnamon sugar. Just the scent of it had my mouth watering. I hoped it would do the same for Jane. I imagined there weren't many opportunities to eat amazing pie in the forest.

I walked away from the stores and houses and entered the forest, following the main path that cut through the trees. I skulked around for a bit, making my presence known and wafting the smell of pie around in the hope of getting Jane's taste buds stimulated.

As I moved deeper into the forest, the path vanished, and the light faded. My foot caught in a hidden tree root, and I gasped as the pie almost flipped from my hand in my attempt to stay upright.

"If you're having trouble keeping hold of the pie, I have a spare mouth," Wiggles said.

"Keep walking. You're not having this pie." I checked inside the pie box. It had gotten shaken around but still looked edible.

"I'm just saying, four legs are better than two. And I'm closer to the ground, so I can watch out for holes and roots." He raced off and returned a moment later with a huge branch sticking out of his mouth and nudged me with his nose.

"Since when do you play stick?" I looked down at the crumbling, moss covered branch.

He jabbed the stick into my leg.

"Ouch! Fine." I went to take it from him.

Wiggles held on tight and growled.

"You don't want to play?"

He jabbed me again.

"If you keep doing that, I might find somewhere unpleasant for that stick to go."

Wiggles shook his head.

I placed the pie down carefully and caught hold of the branch again. He almost yanked me from my feet with the strength of his tug.

I pulled back and held on as Wiggles shook his head. "Jeez, have you been on the *Hellhound Bulk Up*

Diet?"

His gaze went to the pie.

"Nooooo, not a chance. Apple pie is only going to give you a pot belly, not muscles." I shook the stick to get his attention back on me.

Wiggles tossed his head to the side, sending me flying.

I pitched backwards and landed on my butt, right on top of the pie box. I glowered at him as I wiped dirt and leaves off my black jeans. "You did that deliberately. That's the last game of tug I play with you."

Wiggles spat out the stick and sat next to me, looking at the squashed pie. "I thought I'd try being a regular dog for a few minutes. You know, try it on for size."

"How's that working out?" I inched up the pie box lid. It was ruined.

"Not so great." His nose edged toward the pie. "That does not look so good."

"Nothing would look good once I've sat on it."

"I should eat it. It's a shame to let good pie go to waste."

"You're not getting any of this." I dug my finger into the pie and ate a piece. "It still tastes great."

Wiggles watched me with narrowed eyes as I tried to reassemble the pie. "What do you know about this wild woman we're badly stalking?"

"Not much. Jane is basically a mystery. For as long as I can remember, she's lived in these woods."

"What powers does she have?"

"I've never seen her do anything with magic, but she must be able to look after herself alone out here. I'm guessing she draws her power from nature, which is why she enjoys spending so much time in the forest."

"Huh! Well, it looks like the pie's not working on drawing her out. Maybe she's allergic to apples," Wiggles said. "We should eat it."

I looked around the densely packed trees. "You could be right. Maybe Jane doesn't like apple pie." I pulled open the lid and broke off a piece of crust. Despite its sad-looking crushed appearance, it was the best I'd ever had.

Wiggles whined and pawed the ground.

I broke off a small piece for him and cut three slices with my pen knife.

Wiggles made short work of his pie. "Let's try me being a regular hound again." He nosed the stick toward me.

"If you say so." I grabbed the stick and threw it.

Wiggles raced off as I munched on my pie. I leaned back against a tree as I waited for him to return. Jane would definitely hear Wiggles crashing around the woods. Even if she didn't like pie, she'd come to check out the noise. From the little I knew of her, she was protective of these trees.

I'd eaten most of my slice when I heard a faint rustle in the bushes to my right. It was far too delicate to be Wiggles. I kept eating. I didn't want to startle Jane by letting her know I was aware of her presence.

Wiggles raced back with the stick.

I grabbed it and leaned forward. "Be discreet. I think someone is watching us."

Wiggles jumped around and scanned the trees.

I shook my head. I shouldn't have bothered. "Go fetch." I threw the stick for him again.

Wiggles raced off, his tongue hanging out and his tail up.

I sensed I was being watched. Unlike Wiggles, I didn't look around to see who it was but nudged the pie farther away with my foot.

A large, matted-haired head appeared around the side of a huge pine tree. A pair of intense dark eyes looked at me without blinking.

I nodded at Jane. "There's pie here if you want it. I can't eat a whole one my own."

Jane's head disappeared. A few seconds later, she stepped out from behind the tree. She was dressed in brown, blending perfectly with the forest. Her long, dark hair was in dreadlocks down to her waist, and her cheeks were smeared with dirt.

"What are you doing in my forest?" Her voice sounded croaky as if she didn't use it often.

"The forest is for everyone in Willow Tree Falls. I'm here simply enjoying some pie. I'm happy to share."

Jane's gaze darted around the forest as if hunting for some sort of trap.

"It's just Wiggles and me. I'm sure you've heard him crashing around. He won't bother you. He's awfully interested in your piece of pie, though, so you'd better be quick if you want any."

She nodded swiftly. "He talks."

"He does. He's a hellhound."

Jane backed up a step.

"Don't worry. He's a harmless hellhound. He's my pet."

Wiggles ran over and eyed Jane. He spat out the stick. "Just don't tell anybody else that. Is that piece of pie mine?" He went to grab the slice set aside for Jane.

I scooped it up. "I told you this is for…" I glanced at Jane. I couldn't use the made-up name Dazielle had given her.

"Suki. And you're my guests in this forest." Defiance flashed in her eyes.

I nodded. "Very well, Suki. We'll be your guests. Perhaps you'd like to join me?"

After looking around again, Suki walked over slowly, giving Wiggles a wide berth. She grabbed the pie and backed away before settling lightly on top of a fallen tree trunk, looking ready to flee if anything startled her.

I gave her a moment to calm down and let the apple pie work its magic.

"It's good pie," she muttered.

"The best. I'm guessing you don't get into Willow Tree Falls too often to sample anything from Sprinkles."

"I do. From the dumpster."

"The dumpster?"

"Patti throws away anything that spoils. Sometimes, she leaves a bag by the side of the dumpster. It's always got good stuff in it, edible stuff. I take what I want and leave the rest for anybody else."

Wiggles dropped the stick and stared at Suki. "There's a bag of cakes left out every night behind Sprinkles? Why did nobody tell me?"

"Because you don't need any more cake," I said.

Wiggles growled at me. "I do. What else don't I know about? Maybe Brogan leaves a pile of puddings behind his place. Or I could get free pizza for life if Tate does the same at Mystic Mushroom."

I groaned. "I'm not letting you out dumpster diving in the middle of the night."

"It's not a problem. I'll let myself out."

Suki laughed quietly. "They're good to me, the local residents. I think they look out for me."

I felt a slither of sympathy for Suki. Even if she did get left treats, it couldn't be much fun hunting for your food out of the trash. I glanced at Wiggles. He hunted in the trash for fallen treasures all the time and was thriving.

"I saw you at the solstice celebrations," I said.

"I saw you as well, sleeping in my forest."

"It's a safe place to sleep."

"Usually it is. I don't like it when there are so many non-magicals around. They have no respect for the place. They make noise and leave litter. It's disrespectful."

"Were there many in the forest that night?"

"A few. I kept out of their way." Suki looked over her shoulder. "They're not right in the head, some of them. Just today, there was a guy in the marsh making all sorts of noise. He kept cursing and falling over like he didn't have a clue what he was doing. He was stabbing a stick into the ground as if he was looking for something he'd lost. He gave up in the end after he pitched headfirst into the marsh. He came out looking like a swamp beast."

I grinned. That must have been James eagerly following my suggestion to hunt for the ring. "I don't suppose he found anything useful during his search?"

"Other than a few unpleasant marsh-borne diseases, I doubt it." Suki shared a small smile with me.

"A few people have mentioned seeing you on solstice night."

"I was around. It's hard to stay out of people's way when it's so busy."

"You don't need to stay out of the way. You'd have been welcome to join in."

"I hate crowds. They're too tiring."

"Sometimes it's nice to have company, especially on a special night like the solstice."

"Maybe. I celebrate in my own way."

I nodded. Parties weren't for everyone. "Did you see any journalists that night?"

Her gaze flicked to me before drifting away. "You're investigating the dead one in your cemetery?"

"Yes, I'm trying to figure out who hurt Nick."

"I didn't see him."

"Not even once? Nick was around a lot interviewing people, taking pictures, and talking to the camera. Around midnight, he was talking to a bunch of women wearing unicorn horns. That would have been hard to miss."

Suki finished her pie and licked the crumbs off her fingers. "I don't remember that." She jumped to her feet as if eager to leave.

"You can have another piece of pie if you'd like."

She eyed the pie greedily. "Maybe a small piece."

I cut a generous slice and handed it to her. "Why do you live in the forest?"

"It's better that way. It's easier. People think I'm weird."

"Everyone's weird in Willow Tree Falls."

She shrugged. "I'm weirder than most."

"Any time you want to come in for a coffee, I'm always around. You're welcome at Cloven Hoof. I don't think I've ever seen you there."

"You won't. The forest gives me everything I require. I serve it, and it nourishes me."

Suki talked in a way that suggested she protected the forest and felt responsible for it. If that was so, that made her a wood nymph. But she couldn't be a wood nymph; they were tiny. They rarely grew to more than four feet in height. She was at least six-foot five and broad in the shoulders and hips. My mom would have said she had hips for childbearing.

Suki looked at me intently. "Have you got any idea who killed Nick?"

"I've no idea. Well, I have a few ideas but no evidence. You're sure you didn't see anything that night?"

She scuffed the ground with her foot. "I knew his family."

I stared at her in surprise. "You did? I thought they moved away a long time ago."

"Nick Saunders, that was his name?"

"That's right."

She shrugged and nodded. "I know them. I remember his grandparents."

"But that would make you…" I stared hard at Suki. If she knew Nick's grandparents, that must make her at least eighty years old.

"I knew them but didn't like them. They were always invading my forest and seeking things that didn't belong to them."

"What sort of things?"

"Objects containing magic. Things they had no right to own. Some they kept, and some they sold. I made it my job to keep things like that out of their way whenever I could, but they kept hunting for more. I didn't get that sense about Nick, though. He seemed like a good person."

"So, you did meet Nick?"

Suki looked away. "I didn't say that. I never spoke to him."

"You were close to him. You must have seen him and seen how he interacted with others to consider him a good person."

She twisted a dreadlock around one finger. "Maybe. I was curious. I sensed his magic, but I realized he had no idea of his power. It's unusual for someone with magic not to feel it when they come to somewhere like Willow Tree Falls."

"Nick definitely felt something. When I met him, he could see the demon I carried. He didn't know what it was. Maybe coming here awakened his abilities."

Suki nodded. "Perhaps. It's too late for him now, though. It's a shame. I was sorry to hear of his death. Us magic users need to look out for those who need help."

"If you don't mind me asking, what exactly are you?"

She flashed me a nervous smile. "You probably already know. I look a bit different to others of my kind."

"Well, I'd have guessed you're a wood nymph."

Suki nodded. "You'd guess right."

"But you're…" I looked her over.

"Enormous. I know. I never stopped growing. It was such an embarrassment to my parents. When I shot to over five foot tall, they started worrying about me. I kept getting bigger and bigger. Eventually, my dad was so convinced Mom had had an affair with a giant that they split up. I'm sure that wasn't true. They were ashamed of me. I could only handle so much teasing before it became too much. I decided the best thing to do was stay out of people's way. No more pointing fingers and people whispering behind my back about my freakish size."

It sucked that people could be so needlessly cruel. Suki seemed like a good person. "I'm sorry to hear you were bullied. You don't need to hide now, though. If anyone says an unkind word to you, you can give them a backhander and send them flying. That will make other people think twice."

Suki shook her head. "I'm not a violent person unless my forest is being threatened. I don't think I could hurt anyone."

"Then ask me. I'm happy to bang heads together if people say unkind things. You don't have to hide, not anymore."

She looked around the forest and sighed. "It doesn't feel like hiding. Besides, I need to stay here and protect the forest. There are too many people who've been poking around lately. I wasn't sure what that journalist was looking for in the marsh, but if he found it and reported the information to others, it will bring more people. People mean damage to my trees. I can't have that. I need to keep everything safe and protected."

"What are you protecting?"

Suki worried her bottom lip with her teeth. "The secrets in the forest."

"Do those secrets have anything to do with the objects containing magic you mentioned?"

She looked around the trees. "I shouldn't say."

"It could help in my search for Nick's killer. He was asking about a ring that had power. If my hunch is right, he's not the only one looking for that ring. Maybe he got too close to it or even found it."

"Oh dear, this is terrible." Suki paced backwards and forward. "I never thought it would come to this."

My heartbeat sped up. "What? Do you know about the ring?"

She nodded, her expression glum. "It should never have happened. There are so many objects hidden in the forest. Normally, I'm on top of it. I do a daily check to make sure everything is where it should be. With the solstice celebrations and so many people about, it felt so stifling. There were times when I didn't want to leave my home. I stayed hidden inside because it was so hectic, and I couldn't face being spotted and laughed at."

"Why is missing a day of checks such a bad thing?"

Suki turned her guilt-filled eyes to me. "One of the objects went missing. I was horrified when I went to its location and it was gone."

"What was taken?"

Suki hung her head. "It was a ring. Many of the items I watched over had been collected by Nick's family. Some they stored in the forest for their own use. I took them when they weren't around and hid them. Of course, they were furious, but they never knew who took the objects. They asked me about it a couple of times, but I pretended I didn't know anything. Then they got evicted from Willow Tree Falls, so I didn't need to worry about them. Instead, I simply guarded the objects they'd left behind to make sure no one else abused them. I knew the forest would keep everything safe."

"You made yourself an unofficial guardian of these objects? You keep them safe, so they don't fall into the wrong hands?"

She nodded. "Yes, it always worried me that things with so much power could corrupt. Now, it looks like that's what has happened. That nice young man found the ring and was killed because of it. It's all my fault."

"Nick's death isn't your fault. He shouldn't have been looking for something with that much power. The only person to blame is whoever killed Nick to get their hands on this ring."

Suki wrung her hands and paced some more. "I was foolish. I let the situation get on top of me. I'm not as young as I used to be, and keeping tabs on all the objects is getting too much. I was hoping I'd have an apprentice by now, but it never happened. I'm all alone. Besides, who would want to work with me?"

Poor Suki. She had zero self-belief and now blamed herself for Nick's death. "Lots of people. You're unique. A giant wood nymph is something special. You should embrace your difference."

"That's easy for you to say." She gestured at her hulking form. "I scare most people."

"Hey, you're looking at a witch who lives with a demon inside of her. You won't meet many people like me."

Her gaze ran over me, and she smiled tentatively. "Maybe we're not so different."

"Exactly. And, since we are so similar, I bet you also notice when someone's not being straight up with you."

Suki looked at me out of the corner of her eye. "What if I do?"

"Well, you'll notice those little tells and the things they do when they're lying. My sister, for example, twitches her nose when she's concealing something. It's such a giveaway. She's been doing it since we were kids."

Suki nodded. "I might notice things like that."

"And you might also notice when someone is trying not to draw attention to themselves or maybe when they're watching someone else."

She turned to face me. "I didn't see anything like that when Nick was killed."

I sat up straight. "But you saw something?"

She stared intently through the trees in the direction of the stone circle. "I saw…"

"What? What did you see?"

"At the stones. It was late. Most of the people had gone." Suki shook her head. "I was wandering around, seeing what people had left behind and tidying up their mess. It makes me so mad to see how little regard non-magicals have for the place."

"Is that when you saw Nick?"

Suki nodded. "He was taking pictures and walking around."

"Was he alone?"

"For a while." Suki's bottom lip trembled. "Then someone ran out of the shadows."

"Did you see who it was?"

"No, they were dressed in black. Nick didn't see them coming. They knocked him over the head."

"He was attacked inside the stone circle?" That would explain the lack of blood at the cemetery.

Suki nodded. "Nick hit the ground hard. Whoever it was, they whacked him over the back of the head several times. He wasn't meant to get up from that."

"The killer moved his body?"

"They must have, but I didn't see. I ran off but then came back. By then, Nick had gone. I went to take a look but couldn't see anything. I expect, if you shift some dirt, you'll find blood."

"What did they do with Nick's body?"

"I didn't see how they moved him."

My hands balled into fists. "Someone went to a lot of trouble to conceal their tracks. Was it a man or a woman?"

"I can't say. Most likely a man. Nick was a well-built guy."

I noticed a flush on Suki's cheeks. It looked like she had a small crush on our dead journalist. "What time was this?"

"Really early in the morning. It must have been around one o'clock. Nearly everyone was gone. There were a few people sleeping, but they didn't wake up. Nick was the only one awake."

"It was a risk to drag his body from here to the cemetery. It must be a quarter of a mile. They'd need to be strong to do that."

"Which makes me think it was a man," Suki said.

"Most likely. It could be James, Nick's journalist friend."

"If you mean the other guy who's been covering the solstice celebrations, then they aren't friends," Suki said. "I overheard them arguing. Nick was furious and telling the other guy to keep his nose out, and it was none of his business."

"Was he talking about the solstice? He didn't want James interfering with his reporting?"

"I don't know, but the other guy told Nick to watch his back."

I picked pie crumbs off my shirt as I considered what Suki had told me. The more I heard about James, the less I liked him. Assuming he survived his experience in the marsh, I needed to talk to him again.

"I think he's involved," Suki said. Her gaze went to the remaining pie.

"Me too. Thanks, Suki." I cut up the remaining pie and shared it between the three of us. James had just jumped to the top of my suspect list. It was time to quiz this smug journalist again and get the truth out of him.

Chapter 13

After leaving Suki in the forest, I headed home with Wiggles to get some sleep. Not that I'd gotten much. I'd tossed and turned thinking about the magic ring, Nick's body being moved from the stone circle, and who could have done it.

I dragged myself out of bed just after dawn. I needed a hearty breakfast and a strong mug of coffee if I was going to face the day and not kill anybody.

Wiggles was still asleep as I pulled on my boots and grabbed my keys. I nudged him gently with the toe of my boot.

He raised his head and blinked up at me blearily. "Is there an emergency?"

"It depends if you consider eating breakfast an emergency."

He jumped to his feet and shook out his fur. "I consider it an emergency. Why the early start?"

"Because we need to get this mystery figured out and fast. We can't have everyone in Willow Tree Falls thinking the Crypt family had anything to do with Nick's murder. Whoever moved the body might have been trying to implicate someone in the family, and that's unacceptable. I need to find James again and see what he knows. He definitely had it in for Nick."

Wiggles eyed me suspiciously. "Breakfast first, though, right? Otherwise, I'm going back to sleep."

"Breakfast first. I'll treat you to something from Unicorn's Trough."

"Now you're talking." Wiggles barged ahead of me and ran down the stairs. "Hurry up."

I shook my head and grinned as I locked the door, walked down the stairs and through Cloven Hoof. It was another bright, sunny day, although chilly, as the sun hadn't long risen. I strolled through the quiet streets, enjoying the calm that always came before the bustle as the stores opened their doors and everyone turned out for the early shift.

Unicorn's Trough opened at six, and I knew Brogan would have breakfast on the go.

There were several other people in the cafe when we entered. I nodded at Brogan, who was chatting to another guy at the counter.

I settled at a table by the window and perused the menu.

"I'm having hash browns," Wiggles said, "two rounds of bacon, some maple syrup pancakes, and a side order of waffles."

"Not a chance. I'll order you a breakfast special, but that's it."

Wiggles checked the specials board. "I can live with that. Ask for extra toast."

Brogan strolled over, a smile on his stubbled face. "I don't usually see you here this early."

"I've got lots to do today."

He raised his dark eyebrows. "If it has anything to do with suggesting our out of town journalists visit any more unusual tourist hotspots, like the marsh, you might like to re-think that." Brogan nodded toward the counter. "That guy has some serious issues with you."

I looked back to the counter. I hadn't recognized him at first, but it was James. "Oh, he must have misunderstood me. I told him to stay away from the marsh. It's a terrible place. No one goes there."

Brogan grinned. "Sure you did. What will it be?"

I placed an order for two breakfast specials. Brogan filled a coffee mug for me before strolling off to put the order in with the kitchen.

I watched as James hopped from his stool at the counter and paid for his breakfast. He turned and froze when he saw me, his cheeks flushing red and his eyes narrowing. He stalked over and glared down at me.

"Good morning," I said sweetly.

"You made me look like an idiot yesterday." James jammed his fisted hands on his hips, making him look anything but macho.

"Why, what did you do?"

"You knew going into the marsh was a wild goose chase. Admit it. There was never a ring there. You wanted to make me look stupid."

"I'm thinking you probably don't need any help with that."

James scowled at me. "I've ruined a pair of my favorite suit pants."

"Then you really are dumb. Why would you wear a suit to go into a marsh?"

"I didn't know it was going to be an actual full-on marsh. The kind of place that sucks your feet in and threatens to drown you if you don't watch where you're going, complete with slime and goodness knows what lurking below the surface and making weird gurgling, burping sounds."

"Then I wouldn't have called it a marsh. I thought you were going to wear waders?"

"That idiot Jenny couldn't find any. I had to make do with wellies, and the disgusting water was soon over the top of them. I poked around there for hours looking for some signs of recent disturbance. There was nothing. That's because there was never anything to find, was there?"

I tilted my head from side to side. "How about this? I'll tell you the truth about the ring if you share what you've learned about it."

His frown deepened, but there was a glint of excitement in his eyes. "Why would you do that?"

"Because I think that ring is connected to your friend's murder. Didn't you say you wanted an exclusive story?"

James's jaw dropped. He snapped it quickly shut. "You think someone killed him for this ring? But it's not even real."

"You seemed to think it was real enough yesterday to go hunting around the marsh for it."

He shrugged and gestured to the chair opposite me. I nodded, and he sat down. "It's a journalistic hunch. And Nick was so convincing about this ring. I got the sniff of an exclusive story and decided to follow it. I figured the ring was an old heirloom. If nothing else, I might earn a bit of money if I discovered it and printed a decent story. Or I could even sell it if I couldn't sell the information."

"You don't think there's any truth that the ring has some kind of magic power?"

James chuckled as he played with the salt and pepper pots on the table. "Doubtful, but I'm willing to keep an open mind. There are always crackpot publications willing to buy a story about mythical objects or strange creatures that are spotted. You can earn a couple of hundred for snapping a blurry shot of Big Foot. Actually, you might be able to help me with that very thing. I've had a few people report seeing a yeti in the forest."

"A yeti!" My thoughts flew to Suki. "There are no yetis here."

"You've never seen some kind of Big Foot character lurking around the woods? Someone said it had dreadlocks and fur all over its body. It's supposed to be over ten feet tall, a real beast, but most likely, some homeless guy who needs a bath and a change of clothes."

I kept my expression as neutral as possible. "Nope, I've never seen anybody like that in the forest." Suki would be devastated if anybody thought she looked like a yeti or even a harmless homeless bum.

"I figured it was a long shot. I want to gather as many stories as possible while I'm here to make it worth the while. After the story runs in today's news about the solstice, I need to follow-up with a few other things. Nick's death is top of my list, but I was hoping this ring mystery and the story of the yeti might be worth pursuing."

I shrugged. "Neither the ring nor the yeti mystery sound promising."

"You said you'd share what you know about this ring. I've told you what I know. Now, it's your turn."

I decided to give him the barest of information, just enough to show willingness. "I've never seen this ring, so I don't know if it's even real. All I've heard is that people think it's powerful."

James's eyes narrowed further as if he was trying to work out if I was yanking his chain. "You're telling me you actually believe a ring can give someone superpowers?"

"I never said superpowers."

"It sounds to me like a case of simple greed. Someone's got their eye on a bit of gold and wants to make money. They attach some nonsense myth to it in the hope of bumping up the offers."

"That could also be true. The ring is old. Old things can be valuable. I'm guessing Nick thought he was onto something when he heard about the ring and decided to look into it while he was here."

James leaned back in his seat and crossed his arms over his chest. "I figured it had to be something boring like that. That's not a story."

"Was it another story you and Nick argued over?"

James frowned. "We never argued."

"You didn't tell the truth about you being friends. Rachel told me you were rivals in business. I also heard you were seen arguing with Nick the night of the solstice and told him to keep his nose out of your business."

James shrugged. "That's how we rolled. Journalism is like that. You have to be at the top of your game or you're forgotten about. There's always somebody else right behind you, wanting to claim the story and put their name on the by-line. There's no harm in it."

"There is if Nick was killed by you."

James's laugh was sharp. "Yeah, right. I wouldn't kill for a story."

"Maybe you would if your career was on the line."

He placed his hands flat on the table and glared at me. "My career is perfect. I'm heading straight for the top as I've always planned. Hanging around Willow Tree Falls and reporting the murder of some second-rate journalist isn't getting me my breakthrough story. And boring pieces to camera about a bunch of eccentrics dancing around stones and making up nonsense about mythical rings is the stuff of local journalism."

Whoops, it looked like I'd touched a nerve. "You want to make the big time?"

"I will make the big time. I'm almost there."

"If this ring myth has any truth to it, that would be a story and a half."

James's lips thinned to an unpleasantly ugly line. "Is it true or not? Or do you spin lies and nonsense about a ring to lure in the tourists?"

I was getting bored with James and his thinly veiled ambitions. "It's nonsense. Don't believe anything you hear about it."

"Maybe you're concealing the truth from me because it is valuable. Maybe you've got the ring. Maybe you took it from Nick and killed him to get your hands on it."

"You're over-stretching your journalistic license by going that far. I live here. If there was a powerful ring, I'd know about it."

"Maybe not. Nick could have arrived with new information. Information you killed him for."

This conversation was not going the way I'd planned. James had turned the tables on me and was accusing me of killing Nick. "I don't need a ring to give me power."

"What are you, the mayor? I thought it was that overweight guy with the hideous beard."

"Our mayor doesn't have a hideous beard." It was a huge, well-oiled beard, the kind you could lose a sandwich in, but Mannie was proud of his beard.

positive and strong. It brings out their best qualities. That's a front. What the ring actually does is absorb the abilities of the wearer. Any magic user who has it will initially get a burst of power and become strong. That's a short-term benefit. What the ring wants is to lure you into a false sense of security and make you believe it's doing you good. Only then does it leach your power. That's why it's so strong. Over thousands of years, that ring has absorbed small amounts of individual magic users' abilities."

"For what purpose?"

"Nobody knows who made the ring. Its original purpose has been lost. Perhaps it was never intended to do that and malfunctioned. You shouldn't go anywhere near it. It will affect your abilities. It could also make Frank stronger, and nobody wants that."

I shuddered as Frank stirred at the mention of his name. "I definitely don't want that. I've been having a few problems with Frank."

Brogan nodded, his expression serious. "I did hear about the chase through the streets. Your sister is okay?"

"She's fine, but it took Tilly a serious amount of effort to get Frank to submit. I couldn't control him."

"That must be... unsettling."

"You could say that." Brogan knew all about tricky abilities. His ancestors were vampires, and he was the long-lived offspring of a human and vampire coupling. He rarely talked about it, but Brogan had his own demons to master.

"Best you leave this ring alone."

I ate some of my delicious breakfast as I considered my options. What Brogan said was sensible. If this ring was as powerful as he claimed, I didn't want to be anywhere near it. I definitely never wanted Frank to get his demon claws on it and use it for nefarious means, like getting revenge on Tilly or finally getting to Aurora. But what if this ring was the solution to Nick's murder? Maybe the killer still had possession of the ring. Find the ring, find the killer.

I sighed. It could also be a huge distraction. Nick could have been killed after an argument that went wrong, and the ring was as mythical as King Arthur.

Brogan tapped the back of my hand and smiled. "It looks like you've still got some work to do before you find the answers to those questions rolling around your head."

I nodded. "I do, but thanks for the advice on the ring."

"Proceed with caution." Brogan stood and drained his mug of coffee. "If you need any more advice or simply another nice breakfast, you know where I am." He winked at me before walking away.

"You should marry him," Wiggles said as he looked up from his empty plate.

I arched an eyebrow. "Where did that come from?"

"Brogan makes the best breakfast."

"Which isn't exactly grounds for a perfect marriage."

"All good relationships have to have a solid basis. The guy who makes a killer breakfast has to be in

HELL OF A WITCH

your top five. And he isn't too shabby with the puddings."

I watched Brogan serving more customers. He was a decent guy, solid and dependable, and he had a flirty side. Wiggles was right; his breakfasts were amazing. But I wasn't husband hunting, I was suspect hunting. And right now, I had a whole heap of suspects and no glue to make any of them stick.

Chapter 14

Following a luxuriously long time spent at Brogan's, I headed to Angel Force to report my suspicions about James. Dazielle wasn't in, so I left her a note to let her know that Nick's body had been moved, and he'd been killed in the stone circle. I also made a few notes about the possible ring link.

As I headed back along the main street, I spotted Rachel walking into the Ancient Imp.

I peered through the window and saw her sitting at the bar. A moment later, Petra Duke served her an enormous bright red cocktail, complete with a lit sparkler and tiny pink umbrella.

"That had better be a non-alcoholic cocktail," I said to Wiggles.

"Whatever it is, it looks good," Wiggles said as he propped himself up next to me on the windowsill. "I could do with one of those."

"You're right. We should get our own." I pushed open the door and entered the bar.

Petra nodded at me as I approached the bar, her long dark, silver-streaked hair piled up on her head. "It's a little early to see you in here."

"I was just passing and fancied a drink."

"What will it be?"

"The usual lemon water." I glanced at Rachel and arched an eyebrow. "You must have gotten out of the wrong side of the bed if you're starting so early with a boozy breakfast." I nodded at the cocktail.

"Oh, this." Rachel's cheeks flushed. "I'm still grieving over Nick. Losing my sweetheart has taken a lot out of me."

I stared at her stomach. "It's all fruit juice, I suppose?"

Rachel pushed the glass away. "It's nothing, a little pick me up."

"Nothing alcoholic?"

Petra snorted a laugh as she passed me my drink. "There's enough alcohol in that cocktail to fell an elephant."

I looked back at Rachel. "Is that so? That can't be good for you and the baby."

Petra grabbed the cocktail and yanked it out of Rachel's hand. "You never told me you're pregnant."

Rachel's gaze dropped to the floor. "It was a mistake."

I narrowed my eyes. "The drink or the baby?"

Rachel looked up at me and scowled. She gestured to Petra. "That's my drink. I'm having it, and I won't be doing anybody any harm."

Petra looked at me for support, and I shook my head. "Maybe I'll give you a lemon water, instead."

"I don't want lemon water. I want my cocktail. That's what I paid for, and that's what I'm going to have," Rachel said.

Petra shook her head. "It's not right. I refuse to serve you."

"It is right." Rachel leaned over the bar. "I'm not pregnant."

Petra looked down at Rachel's decidedly flat stomach. "Well, you don't look it. Maybe you're too early to show a baby bump."

"There'll never be a baby bump because I'm not carrying a baby. Now, give me my drink."

Petra placed the cocktail back on the bar and slid it toward her.

I watched as Rachel took a huge gulp of the cocktail. "Why did you lie to me about being pregnant?"

Rachel glanced around the bar. "Not here." She gestured for me to follow her to a quiet corner. We sat at the table, and I waited for her to continue.

She looked at me and sighed. "I never meant to lie. I did want a baby with Nick. I was trying so hard, but he wasn't taking our relationship seriously. I had to find a way to make him grow up."

"So, you faked being pregnant?"

"I thought it would be good for us. It would give Nick something positive to focus on and stop his obsession over beating James. It was so tiring. Every day he'd complain about James and how good he was at his job and how he always beat him to the best stories. Not only was it tiring, but it was boring. Nick wasn't focusing on us. I decided, if we had a baby together, it would make him do that. It would make him realize how important I was to him."

"What were you going to do when he realized you weren't pregnant?"

"It would have happened. I was taking every opportunity I could to get pregnant by him."

I wrinkled my nose. "I get the picture, but it would still have been suspicious if the baby didn't arrive for another twelve months."

"I'd have figured out something and concealed the truth. Nick was so busy that he probably wouldn't have noticed if I got the dates messed up. Anyway, by then, it would have been too late. Even if he found out I'd lied to him, we'd have been having a baby together. That would have kept us together and made him take our relationship seriously."

That sounded like a terrible way to keep a relationship going, lie to a guy, trick him into thinking he's going to be a dad, and then get yourself pregnant. There was a recipe for an unhappy life. "What makes you think he didn't know you were lying to him?"

"Nick didn't have a clue. He trusted me."

"Are you certain he didn't find out?" It sounded like an excellent motive for murder. If Nick had figured out how devious Rachel was being and dumped her, she was spiteful enough to get her revenge. I imagined Rachel wasn't the kind of woman who was used to being dumped.

"No, it was nothing like that. I'll admit Nick was being on the cool side with me in the last few weeks. That was all the more reason I needed to get pregnant. I had to give him a reason to stay with me."

"Or you could have accepted you weren't right for each other and moved on to somebody else. It sounds like you need someone with lots of ambition. Have you ever thought about dating James? He has a tenacious way about him." He also had a hole in his pristine pants, thanks to Wiggles, and squealed like a frightened mouse when scared.

Rachel scowled at me. "James is ambitious. I have looked at him a few times, but he made it clear he's not interested. He said something gross about sloppy seconds not being his style, whatever that means."

Wow, Rachel was something else. She'd decided to stay with Nick because James didn't want her and then faked a pregnancy to get Nick to stay with her. She was the girlfriend from hell. She'd fit in nicely in the demon prison. I should offer her a one-way ticket.

"Since you lied about the baby, you might also have lied about the rivalry between James and Nick."

She shook her head. "Absolutely not. They hated each other."

"Prove it."

Rachel glared at me over her almost empty cocktail glass. "Why should I?"

"Because I'm investigating your boyfriend's murder, and you've not been telling the truth.

Therefore, you're unreliable and have a motive for wanting Nick dead."

"I do not. I've never wanted Nick dead. Well, maybe I wanted him hurt sometimes when he wouldn't buy me what I wanted or refused to take me to my favorite restaurant. But dead, never." She slurped the glossy cherry off her umbrella stick.

"I don't believe you. I should take you to the station for further questioning."

Rachel scowled at me. "Fine, I can prove it. I'll call Nick's editor, Ivan. He worked with Nick and James. They were vying for the same staff position at the paper. He'll show you I'm telling the truth. He knows all about their rivalry." She pulled out her mobile and stared at it for a few seconds. "It's so strange. This thing is always going on the blink here. You must have a terrible cell signal reception."

I grinned at her. It wasn't the cell signal that was the problem. It was all the magic in the village that messed up the phones. It's why no one used them in Willow Tree Falls. "We have the worst. Barely anyone uses a mobile around here."

She stared at me as though I'd said something obscene. "What a nightmare! How do you check your social media? I'll give it a go and see if I can get through to Ivan."

It took Rachel several attempts, but she finally got the call to connect. "Put me through to Ivan."

I sipped my drink as I watched Rachel's eyes narrow. It looked like bad news. "No, I don't believe he's out. He always speaks to me. It's urgent. Tell him it's Rachel Fortesque."

I glanced down at Wiggles and winked at him. He shook his head and settled his muzzle on his paws as if expecting this would take a long time.

She raised her eyebrows at me and shook her head. "These receptionists are so full of themselves. They act like guard dogs, thinking they have control over you just because they decide whether you get to speak to their boss. It's pathetic."

"I can imagine," I said.

"Ivan, it's Rachel. How are you, sweetie?" She pressed a button and placed the phone on the table.

"Good thanks," Ivan boomed out of the speaker. "How are things with you? I hope Nick's treating you well. Let me know if he's being a bad boy." His chuckle sounded lecherous.

"Oh, I've got some sad news about Nick. He's dead."

Ivan made several spluttering sounds. "What happened?"

"I'm not sure. It's a terrible blow. I'm so distraught." Rachel sniffed loudly and looked at her empty glass.

"You poor thing. I hope you're being looked after."

"I'm managing, but you know what these places are like. Everything takes forever to get going."

My smile felt too much like a snarl, so I pinched my lips together.

"I'll have to find someone to fill Nick's shoes. You've got James with you, haven't you?"

"He's here."

"Well, that's a good thing." Ivan cleared his throat noisily. "In a way, as difficult as this is, it makes it easier for me. I wasn't sure who to pick out of the two of them. They've been fighting for the same spot for months. To be honest, it was getting unpleasant."

Rachel rolled her eyes. "Tell me about it. Nick was obsessed with getting that position. It's all he talked about."

"At least he can't stress about it now. Nick is in a better place. I tell you what. I'll put a nice piece in the paper about him, a memorial to Nick. That way, we won't need to do a whip around in the office for flowers for his funeral."

"That's thoughtful of you," Rachel said. "Nick would have liked that."

"Excellent. I'll confirm James in the staff position and get him to write it."

I almost choked on my lemon water. I did not like to think what James would write about Nick when he was forced to create that piece of fiction.

Rachel looked at me and nodded. "See," she mouthed.

I shrugged. I'd heard enough from the unsympathetic editor and mulled over the remaining suspects as Rachel wrapped up her phone call.

"Is that proof enough for you?" she said. "I told you Nick and James hated each other."

"Hated each other enough for it to lead to murder?"

Rachel frowned. "I don't know about that. They mainly messed up each other's work, playing mean prants that sort of thing."

"You don't think James killed Nick?"

"Killing for a job? That suggests desperation. And although a position on Ivan's paper pays okay, it's not the New York Times."

"If you say so. You've never seen them actually fight?"

"It was always verbal sparring. I imagine the last time either of them had a fist fight, they were in the playground wearing short pants."

"When we spoke at the hotel, you mentioned Nick talked about a ring he was looking for."

"An engagement ring? Did he say something to you about getting me an engagement ring?" Rachel's eyes flashed with a look that had to be desire.

I repressed a sigh. "No, but he talked about his search for a ring while he was here."

Rachel shrugged and looked out the window, her interest vanishing. "I didn't listen to his boring work stories. He said something about an old ring, but I lost interest."

I shook my head. I was not surprised that the only time Rachel listened was when the information related to her bare finger getting a huge rock on it.

"I need to get out of here," Rachel said. "I've had enough of small towns."

"You'd better not go anywhere too soon."

Rachel's eyes narrowed. "Why not?"

"You've proved that you're a liar, and you're deceitful, which suggests you could have had something to do with Nick's death."

"Me! I had nothing to do with it. Can't you tell how upset I am?"

I couldn't. She could turn on the water works when she needed to, but I'd never seen anyone less distressed over losing a loved one.

"Make sure you stick around until you hear otherwise," I said. "You might have more information that's useful to the investigation. After all, you do want to find out who killed Nick, don't you?"

"I guess. If I stay much longer, I'll die of boredom."

"It's better than being dead because someone smacked you over the back of the head. You can survive a few more days here."

Rachel scowled at me. "I can stay a couple more days."

"Tempest, you've got a message from Dazielle," Petra called from behind the bar.

I welcomed the chance to get away from Rachel. I left the table and walked to the bar.

Petra pointed to the snow globe tucked discreetly in one corner. "She says she wants to see you over at the standing stones immediately. When does Dazielle get to order you around?"

"Since we formed a temporary alliance. Can you let her know I'm on my way?"

"Will do," Petra said. "Has this got to do with the dead journalist? You think she's found out who did it?"

I nodded as I hurried to the door with Wiggles by my side. "Let's hope so. Then everything can get back to normal and our… tourists can head on home."

Petra looked over at Rachel. "Here's hoping."

As I hurried away from the Ancient Imp, hope fluttered inside me. Maybe the information I'd passed on from Suki had led Angel Force to the killer. They could have found evidence at the standing stones and were about to make an arrest.

This mystery was about to be solved, and I couldn't be happier not to have to deal with uptight, lying girlfriends and sneaky journalists.

Chapter 15

I slowed as I hurried past Sprinkles on my way to the standing stones. I spotted Auntie Queenie coming out of the bakery with a box of cakes.

Wiggles immediately abandoned my side and raced over to her. He sat neatly in front of Auntie Queenie and raised one paw.

I jogged over to catch up with him. "Are you celebrating?" I pointed to the box.

"There's always a reason for cake." Auntie Queenie looked down at Wiggles. "But you're not getting any."

He whined and nudged her leg with his nose.

She chuckled. "You can stop that. Where are you off to in such a hurry?"

"We're on our way to the stones. Nick was killed there."

Auntie Queenie's eyebrows shot up. "There you go then. That proves my innocence."

I tilted my head to the side. "Not that I think you're guilty, but how come?".

She pursed her lips. "As if I need to prove my innocence to you. But it would make no sense for me to kill someone at the stones and then move the body to the place I spend most of my time. Only an idiot would do that."

"Or maybe you're being extra clever. You could have taken Nick's body to the cemetery, thinking you could conceal him in a grave. Someone disturbed you before you could finish the ghastly deed, and you had to abandon the body." I didn't mean it, not seriously, but it was always amusing to wind up Auntie Queenie.

She jammed one hand on her hip. "As if I would desecrate our cemetery by doing that."

"I'm just trying to think like an angel. They might think that exact thing and haul you in for questioning."

Auntie Queenie puffed out her cheeks. "Then I'm glad I've got all these cakes. It's stressful being a murder suspect. I'll be comfort eating all day at this rate. I might have to take up jogging to shed the extra pounds gained if this doesn't get wound up quickly."

"That's your fault. You shouldn't conceal information."

Auntie Queenie's eyes widened. "What information have I concealed?"

"You were hiding something when I came to breakfast. You wouldn't have said anything about threatening Nick if Uncle Kenny hadn't put his foot in it."

"That's why I always tell him it's best if I do the talking. Don't worry. I've had words with him. He won't be doing that again any time soon."

"That's not really the point. Why hide it if it's not important to this investigation?"

"I didn't do it because I'm guilty of murder. I did worry it made me look bad." Auntie Queenie sighed. "Your uncle is right. I did sort of threaten Nick. He was being so sure of himself. He acted like he knew everything about magic. I only said those things to spook him and give him a little humility."

"What exactly did you do?"

Auntie Queenie looked around, not meeting my gaze. "I might have shown him inside the family crypt."

"Did our ancestors' remains creep him out?"

"Nick said it wasn't the first time he'd seen a pile of old bones."

That didn't seem so bad. We never encouraged non-magicals in the crypts, but he wouldn't have seen anything he shouldn't. "That's it?"

"I might have mentioned the demon prison."

My jaw dropped. She had to be kidding. "Why would you do that?" We always worked so hard to make sure non-magicals had no clue what went on there.

Auntie Queenie waved her hand in the air. "He didn't believe me. Nick thought it was some silly tourist folktale. He said he was surprised I didn't charge him to come into the cemetery, which is actually a good idea. We could make every non-magical who wants to poke around pay to enter. It would help with the upkeep of the prison, and I'd have more money to spend on cake."

"That's an excellent plan," Wiggles said, his gaze fixed on the cake box. "We can start a treat fund for hungry hellhounds."

"We aren't doing that. The last thing we need are hordes of non-magicals traipsing over the graves. Think how much it will irritate the demons. An irritated demon means a tougher job for you."

"We can threaten the demons with it. We'll tell them, if they don't behave themselves, we'll set the non-magicals on them." Auntie Queenie chuckled to herself.

I grimaced. That would certainly work on me. "Is there anything else you've decided not to reveal?"

Auntie Queenie opened the cake box and sniffed. "These do smell lovely. Can I tempt you with one?"

"Go on," Wiggles said. "I'll take two."

"No, stop distracting me with cake." I pushed the lid back down. "What else did you tell Nick?"

"It was nothing serious. I simply suggested he should come back that night. I told him I'd show him a demon."

"Were you being serious?"

She shrugged. "There was something about that young man that intrigued me. For all his bluff and confidence, he had a genuine interest in magic. He wasn't a wide-eyed Goth looking to commune with the Devil or a New Age type smelling of incense. He wanted to believe so badly."

"You sensed his latent magic abilities?"

"I believe so. I was curious to see what he really knew and how far I could push his belief before it became too much."

"Did Nick come back to meet your friendly demon?"

"That's just it; he never showed. I was shocked when his body was discovered in the cemetery. I hoped he hadn't come looking for me and his killer jumped out and got him. I'd feel terrible."

"You were on duty that night, weren't you?"

"That's right. I was there with your uncle Kenny and your mom for part of the night. We kept swapping, so everyone got to have fun at the celebrations."

"Are you sure you didn't see or hear anyone? Someone would have carried him into the cemetery."

"Not a thing. Whoever it was, they were swift and quiet. They brought him in, left him, and vanished. It makes me think they must have magic to be so stealthy. Few people get past me in that cemetery."

"You should be careful. If you were there, the killer might have seen you. You don't want them coming after you if they consider you a threat. They might be worried you saw them."

"What nonsense. One little killer won't stop me."

"Even so, watch your back. I should know more from Angel Force once they've spent time at the site of the murder. If anyone is acting oddly around you or you get the feeling you're being followed, let me know. The killer is still on the loose."

"So long as you don't still think it was me, then I don't really mind being stalked," Auntie Queenie said. "But you need to hurry up and find the killer before I stress eat my way to an early grave."

"That's the plan," I said.

"Good girl." Auntie Queenie pulled a sugared doughnut out of the box and handed it to me. "Make sure you keep those angels off my back. I can't have my reputation tarnished by them trying to put me behind bars."

I grinned at her and bit into the sugared doughnut. "You don't make it easy on me, but I'll do my best." I gave her a wave goodbye as I hurried away, Wiggles glued to my side in the hopes of getting some doughnut.

Auntie Queenie had been foolish encouraging Nick, and she had revealed far too much about what went on in the cemetery. Her conversation with him might have sparked his interest in demons, and he'd asked the wrong person the wrong question and gotten himself whacked over the head.

"You know, it's rude not to share food," Wiggles said.

I passed him a piece of doughnut and brushed sugar from my fingers. "Let's hope the angels have found something useful at the stones. It's time we wrapped up this case and got on with our lives."

"I'm thinking we need a long holiday," Wiggles said, "somewhere hot and sunny."

"You've never liked hot and sunny before."

"Things change. Now, I run hellhound hot. I'm thinking a bit of extra sun will do me good. And I'd like someone cute to rub suntan lotion on my belly."

"I'll think about it. But if you're considering a holiday, you need to get in shape. That means no more doughnuts."

Wiggles grumbled. "Maybe a vacation is a bad idea. Part of the fun on a holiday is you get to eat as much as you like with no one telling you how fat you are."

"You won't get anyone cute to rub your belly if it's too big." We headed up the hill to the standing stones. As we got near, I saw Dazielle and two other angels walking around, looking official.

Dazielle raised her hand when she saw me. "I got your message. We came out here to take a look."

"What did you find?"

"Blood covered over by dirt, just as you said. It looks like Nick was killed here and moved to the cemetery," Dazielle said. "Although I have no clue why they'd want to move him."

"To make it harder for you?"

"If that's the case, it's working," Dazielle said. "Any progress on interviewing people?"

I gave her a quick update as to what Auntie Queenie had told me and the conversations I'd had with Rachel and James.

Dazielle scowled at me. "What your aunt says makes sense. I guess it was a long shot thinking I could pin the murder on a crazy old lady who spends all her time in the cemetery eating cake."

"I'll pass those kind words on to my aunt."

"Maybe you shouldn't," Dazielle said. "As for Rachel, she definitely needs to stick around. She could be lying about more than a fake pregnancy."

"That's my thinking. But would she have the strength to kill Nick and drag his body to the cemetery?"

"It would be a job, and it would be tricky not to be spotted doing it," Dazielle said. "Even though Nick was killed early in the morning, there should have been a few late-night partygoers around. It was a huge risk moving the body."

I looked at the dark stain on the ground uncovered by the angels. "What do you think about the information I left about this mysterious ring? Has that got something to do with this?"

Dazielle twirled her long, blonde braid around her hand. "It might, but I've got no clue about it."

"I spoke to Brogan. He suggested it might be the Ring of Halo."

Dazielle's cheeks paled, and she swallowed loudly. "Let's hope it's not. Journalists do not want to be writing a story about that particular ring."

"It's missing," I said. "Suki, also known by you as Jane, was looking after it in the forest."

"Heavens above! Then it needs to be found and quickly," Dazielle said. "A missing ring and a body being moved that nobody noticed. Someone with magic must be involved. Someone strong."

Uh oh, Dazielle had that look in her eyes. The one suggesting she was making up a new theory that was most likely wrong. "I'm thinking we find the ring, and we find Nick's killer."

"I had an anonymous tipoff come in about someone seen in the woods around the time of Nick's murder," Dazielle said. "I didn't take it seriously at the time. It was so vague, but since the killing took place here, it could be relevant."

"That someone could have been me."

"From the description, I'm sure it was Jane, or rather, Suki. And she's strong and knows a lot about magic. She also had access to the ring and could be lying about it being stolen. Maybe she decided to try it and got in over her head."

This was her genius idea? "No, she didn't do that. She was mortified about the ring going missing."

Dazielle paced around. "I'm onto something here. We're bringing Suki in for questioning."

That was a terrible plan. "She won't be thrilled about that. It took me a while to convince her to come out of hiding when I spoke to her. Suki is never going to agree to leave the forest."

Dazielle's blue eyes gleamed with excitement. "Which is why we're sending a search party in tonight. We're going to flush her out of hiding and make her talk. Suki is involved."

A shiver of shock ran through me. She couldn't be serious. "She's not. I've already talked to her. You don't want to do that. The forest is her home. Suki is fiercely protective of the trees."

"Which means she considered Nick a threat and decided to get rid of him."

"Whoa! Slow down with this crazy theory. Why would she kill someone? She'd just scare him off if he made a nuisance of himself."

"It would have been easy for Suki to wait for an opportunity when it was late and dark and Nick was on his own. He could have gone into the forest earlier in the day and done something to upset her."

"Why point me to the blood stain if she killed Nick? It's too obvious."

"To make us think she's being helpful and throw us off her trail."

"Maybe she is being helpful. Suki was the only one to see the murder take place. She could have kept quiet, and we'd be none the wiser. She's trying to assist us. Don't penalize her for that." The angels were so quick to find an easy target and pin the crime on them. They'd tried to do it to my sister, and now, they wanted to do it to Suki.

"If you're so concerned, you can always assist with the search for Suki." Dazielle glared at me. "After all, we are supposed to be working together."

"I'll help with the search." There was no way they were going to yank a confession out of Suki. I would be here tonight, and I would be helping, but I wasn't helping the angels. I would make sure Suki wasn't dragged in and terrified into confessing to something she didn't do. Just because she was a bit different didn't mean the angels could make her a scapegoat.

"Great. Meet us back here at eight o'clock."

I nodded as I took a final look around. I'd be in the search party, but it wouldn't go the way Dazielle wanted it to go.

"Are you sure I can't have a head torch?" Wiggles walked alongside me as I strolled away from Cloven Hoof.

"You don't need a head torch. It's not even fully dark, and you have those glowing eyes. They must help you see at night."

"I have twenty-twenty vision no matter what time of day or night it is. A head torch would look cool."

"That's debatable." I wanted to make sure I got to the search in plenty of time. My plan was simple; be the first to find Suki and warn her what was going on and give her a chance to get away before the angels got her.

"Just keep focused on what you're doing tonight," I said to Wiggles. "Remember where we last saw Suki. We'll head there and see if we can get her attention. Whoever sees her first warns her what's going on. Then we distract the angels until she's in the clear."

"Got it. These angels won't know what's hit them."

"Don't draw attention to yourself. If they think we're working against them, they might shut us out of the rest of this investigation." I wanted to see this through and make sure the angels didn't make any more blunders. I was also curious about this ring. I didn't want to use it, but it intrigued me.

As we arrived at the stones, there were six angels and Dazielle already assembled. So much for the element of surprise and getting a head start.

I recognized the team of angels. They were all tall, stunningly blonde women with bright blue eyes and perfect skin. For once, they weren't wearing their trademark white but dark brown and black clothes.

Dazielle finished up her conversation and walked over. "I'm glad you could join us. We're about to begin."

"Great. Lead the way."

The angels formed a line. Dazielle led from the middle as we walked into the forest. It was tricky to see all the angels but easy for me to break away without being noticed and head to the place where I'd shared the squashed apple pie with Suki.

A shout came up from the end of the line Wiggles was covering. "I see someone."

All the angels dashed toward the sound of the voice. I stayed where I was and continued on my own. I didn't want to alarm Suki, and I had to hope they were following a false trail; otherwise, she'd be in real trouble.

I spotted movement ahead and sped up. I might be tracking a rabbit, but it would have to be a huge rabbit. "Suki, wait up," I whispered loudly.

I slowed as I tried to catch a glimpse of her. A rough-palmed hand shot out from behind the tree I was passing and grabbed hold of me. Suki slammed me against the trunk. Her eyes were wild, and her whole body shook.

"What's happening? Why are angels in my forest?"

"Listen, you don't have much time. Angel Force thinks you're involved in Nick's murder. They're here to bring you in for questioning."

Suki's bottom lip wobbled. "Why do they think that?"

"We don't have time to talk about it. You need to get out of here. Lie low for a few days until I've figured this out and talked sense into them."

Her dark gaze fixed onto me. "You don't think I had anything to do with it, do you?"

"No, but the angels think they're onto something. Once you're in custody, it will be harder to convince them of your innocence."

"I can't leave my forest." Suki looked around, fear in her eyes. "It won't be safe if I'm not here."

"Which is why you're going to stay hidden. Have you got somewhere safe you can hide?"

She nodded and dropped her hold on me. "I can stay out of people's way if I need to do so."

"Then do it. I'll lead the angels in the opposite direction and give you a chance to get away."

"Thanks, Tempest." Suki raced away into the gloom of the trees.

I watched until I couldn't see her anymore before heading in the direction I'd last heard an angel shout. I side-stepped a huge tree and walked straight into Dazielle.

"What happened to you?" She glared down at me as I backed up a few steps.

"I heard a noise and went to check it out." I resisted the urge to check over my shoulder. "Did you find anything?"

"It was a false alarm. We spooked a deer."

"Great. I mean, better luck next time. Let's keep looking."

Dazielle narrowed her eyes. "I heard you talking to someone."

"It was just Wiggles."

"I don't see him." She looked around. "Where is he?"

"Off hunting for Suki, just like we should be."

Dazielle shook her head. "He was at the other end of the line. I saw the two of you separate when you joined us. What's going on?"

"I've got something," a voice yelled through the trees.

Dazielle opened her mouth as if to say more but then snapped it shut. "We'll discuss this later. Let's go."

We'd discuss nothing if I had my way. Dazielle might not be the brightest angel in the box, but I hadn't fooled her. I hurried after her, worry running through me as we headed in exactly the same direction as Suki had run. She didn't have a big enough head start, and angels could move quickly. Fortunately, the densely packed trees made it impossible for them to take flight; otherwise, it would be easy for them to spot Suki.

The sounds of scuffling and a muffled yelp came through the trees.

"Let's move." Dazielle trotted along in front of me.

As we entered a small clearing, my eyes widened. Suki stood in the middle of the clearing, an angel on either side of her. Her hands were balled into fists and her teeth bared in a terrifying snarl.

"Be careful," Dazielle said as she inched closer. "We don't know what we're dealing with."

"We do," I snapped. "She won't harm you. Suki's a wood nymph."

Dazielle's jaw dropped. "That's impossible. She's gigantic."

"It doesn't matter how big she is. Suki's here as a protector of the forest. She thinks you're a threat to her sanctuary, so she will defend herself."

"She's the threat. Angels, take her down," Dazielle ordered.

"No, wait!" I lunged forward, trying to block the angels' path to Suki.

Dazielle shoved me back. "Stay out of this fight, Tempest. You're not needed."

"Suki, get out of here," I yelled as I watched the angels drop into a fighting stance and extend their wings. They had muscular wings that spanned over eight feet and could break a man's arm with a single swipe.

Suki's panicked gaze went to me as an angel landed on her back. She flicked the angel over her shoulder and kicked dirt in her face before spinning and sucker punching another angel who dared get too close.

"Don't fight," Dazielle said. "It will only make things worse for you."

"Of course she's going to fight. You're attacking her." I silently willed Suki to kick their butts. She did not deserve this treatment.

"It's my forest," Suki gasped. "There's no fighting in my forest."

"Then come quietly," Dazielle yelled.

Suki shoved back an angel who'd tried to grab her. She picked up a huge branch and swung it in a circle around her, the remaining angels scattering as she did so to avoid being pulverized.

"We don't want to hurt you." Dazielle held out her hands, trying to placate Suki, and almost ended up with a head full of splintered wood.

"You're doing a terrible job of proving that," I muttered.

Dazielle glared at me before continuing. "Come quietly, and we'll have no more problems."

Suki threw the branch like a javelin. It slammed into an angel's chest. She charged another angel and barreled her backwards into a tree.

Despite how angry Suki was, I could see her shaking with fear. The angels weren't playing fair. I dodged past Dazielle and ran to Suki. "Calm down. This isn't doing you any—" I flew through the air, punched in the gut by Suki in her blind rage and panic.

The breath slammed from my chest as I hit a tree and thudded to the ground.

I could do nothing but watch as the angels overwhelmed Suki. She was lost under a pile of white feathers and fists.

Dazielle stomped over and glared down at me. "I should arrest you, as well."

"What for?" I struggled to my feet and sucked in air, my lungs feeling almost as bruised as my back.

"You interfered in Angel Force business. You're supposed to be on our side, not helping a murderer escape."

"First off, Suki is not a murderer. As usual, you're getting this wrong. Second, you asked me to be involved because you can't cope with sunburned, hung-over non-magicals complaining about losing their ice cream. And third, I never side with bullies. You didn't need to come here with feathers blazing. Suki's done nothing wrong."

Dazielle scowled at me. "That's for me to decide. Stay out of this. Your work is done on this case."

"What are you talking about? You can't charge Suki just because she lives in the forest and prefers trees to people."

"I will charge her when she confesses." Dazielle turned to the angels, who held Suki firmly between them. "Take her to the station. Get her ready for questioning."

"You're being an idiot," I said to Dazielle. "She's not involved in this. She isn't the murderer."

Dazielle glared at me before walking away.

Wiggles trotted over and licked my hand. "That didn't go so well."

"Where were you when the angels went all Lara Croft on Suki?"

"Watching from a safe distance. I should have brought some popcorn. Those ladies can fight."

I groaned and thumped my head against a tree. "We're not letting them get away with this. The angels can't charge Suki because she's an easy target."

"What's the plan?"

I stared through the trees at the wispy white feathers floating in the breeze. "It looks like we're going to be hanging out with the angels. I'm not going to stop pestering them until they let Suki go."

Chapter 16

My back protested as I jerked awake. I'd been waiting all night at Angel Force's headquarters. Every attempt I'd made to see Suki had been blocked. Dazielle had been serious when she said I was to have nothing more to do with this investigation.

I wished she'd make up her mind. This was the last time I'd do them any favors.

I stretched and stood from the chair I'd been dozing in. The day was brightening outside, and I was in need of a strong coffee to get my brain to register it was morning.

Looking around the quiet waiting room, there was a definite lack of Wiggles. The last time I'd seen him, he'd been dozing by my feet. The door to the room was ajar. He must have slipped out when I was asleep, most likely looking for something to eat.

The angels had been reluctant to let him in, especially after the last time he'd been here and had helped break me out of my cell. They'd even put up a sign outside the front door saying no hellhounds allowed, but I'd negotiated with them, and Wiggles had promised to stay quiet and behave himself if he could stay inside.

I strolled into the reception area and nodded at Sablo, the angel on the desk, before checking outside. There was no sign of Wiggles.

"Lady, I'm going to bite you so hard on your feathery butt that you'll remember me for months." I turned as I heard Wiggles and saw two angels carrying him in a large white mesh net.

"Hey! What are you doing to my dog?" I hurried over, watching with alarm as Wiggles writhed in the net, only succeeding in getting himself more tangled.

They dumped Wiggles on the ground and left him in the net.

One of the angels looked at me and scowled. "You need to keep your hellhound under control."

I knelt and unwound the net from around him. "Where did you find him?"

"Poking his fuzzy nose where it shouldn't be. He stays outside from now on."

They both turned and stalked back into the building.

I pulled the rest of the netting off Wiggles. "What's going on? Why are the angels so mad at you?"

He stood and shook out his fur. "Those pesky angels, I should pluck them like chickens."

"Less plucking, more talking. What were you doing that made them net you?"

Wiggles slid me a sideways glance. "Nothing bad. They left the reception desk unattended for a few minutes. I snuck out back to take a look. I wanted to see how Suki was doing."

I stroked a hand along his back. Other than some ruffled fur, he looked fine. "Did you find her?"

"No, just a lot of angels sitting around doing nothing. It's amazing Willow Tree Falls doesn't fall apart with them in charge of keeping everything safe."

"Sometimes, it does feel like it's falling apart." I sat back on my heels. "You got caught snooping?"

Wiggles grabbed the net he'd been wrapped in and tore a big hole in it with his teeth. "All I was doing was trying to get a cookie. There was a whole plate on the sideboard. No one was touching them. That is a serious crime. I'd reached the plate and had my mouth open when I was covered in this sticky, gross, sweet smelling angel net. They bundled me up and brought me out here."

"Trust you to get caught over cookies. I thought you were doing something noble, not scavenging."

"Consuming unloved cookies is a noble thing to do." Wiggles glared at the closed doors. "I'm telling you it's time to break out Frank. He could have fun with those stuck-up angels, who do not eat cookies that so desperately need a home."

I was almost cranky enough and desperate enough to let Frank out. Being nice to the angels had gotten me nowhere, and now they'd mistreated Wiggles.

Maybe time playing with a demon would make them see things differently.

"Tempest, what's going on?"

I turned and saw Aurora and Auntie Queenie approaching.

"What are you doing here?"

"We heard what happened last night in the forest," Aurora said. "We were worried you might have been arrested, especially after the whole... Frank incident at Tilly's."

"It wasn't me this time," I said. "And sorry about Frank chasing you. I'm glad you got away."

Aurora raised a hand. "No need to apologize. We all let our demons get the better of us at times."

I shared a smile with my little sister. She was always so understanding when it came to my Frank issues. "The angels arrested Suki. Dazielle's got it into her thick head that Suki is involved with Nick's murder."

"First me and then that poor girl," Auntie Queenie said. "These angels are something else."

"If you discount the angels she pounded into the ground, Suki wouldn't hurt anybody," I said.

"You're right there," Auntie Queenie said. "She does a good job looking after the forest. If she has to break a few angel heads to do so, it's understandable."

"She did do a number on a couple of the angels."

"With those angels stamping around, crushing plants, and making a nuisance of themselves, she had a right to defend what she loves."

"Suki does have some awesome moves when she's riled," Wiggles said.

The door to Angel Force opened. Dazielle stepped out, a scowl on her face. "You're needed," she said to me, completely ignoring everyone else.

I folded my arms across my chest. "I thought I was off this case."

Her lips pursed. "You are."

"So, why do you need me?"

Dazielle's scowl deepened. "Suki won't talk. We've been questioning her all night, and she just sits looking in the corner of the room with her back to us."

"Good for her," Auntie Queenie said. "She's a nice girl. You shouldn't mistreat her."

"She's a suspect in a murder investigation." Dazielle's gaze hardened as she looked at Auntie Queenie. "And you need to be careful because you might go back on my suspect list if you start causing problems."

"Then you're as dumb as you are pretty if you do that," Auntie Queenie said.

Dazielle looked momentarily confused by the insult mingled with a compliment. She focused back on me. "Suki will not speak to us before she's spoken to you."

"You've had me waiting here all night," I said. "I could have talked to her at any time."

"Not before we conducted our own interview."

"You've been asking questions for hours, and Suki hasn't said a single word?"

Dazielle sniffed. "Something like that. She asks for tea and crumpets a lot."

"You'd better go in," Aurora said. "It sounds like Suki needs you."

"Yes, go get that poor girl out of there," Auntie Queenie said. "Send her to your mom's for tea and crumpets when she's free. Then you can continue your hunt for the real killer."

Part of me was tempted to drop Dazielle in it and walk away from this mess. The angels had wasted everyone's time, forced me to sleep upright in a hard white chair, and netted Wiggles and tossed him out of the station. But that wouldn't be fair to Suki. I could talk to her, make sure she was calm, and try to get the angels to see sense.

"Lead the way." I waved goodbye to Aurora and Auntie Queenie and headed back into the station for Dazielle. Wiggles remained outside, a glare on his face as Aurora rubbed his belly. He was holding a serious grudge against the angels if a tummy rub didn't improve his mood.

"Any chance of a coffee?" I asked Dazielle.

"No."

We walked past the reception desk, along the corridor, and into a small, white interview room.

Suki jumped from her seat when she saw me. Panic flared in her eyes, and her bottom lip quivered. "Tempest, I'm so sorry about hurting you when we were in the forest. I didn't know what I was doing. I heard your voice but reacted on instinct. It's a wood nymph thing. When we sense danger, we get mad. It's like a momma bear gets protecting her cubs."

I lifted a hand to slow her flood of words. "It's fine. I just have a few bruises."

Suki ducked her head and clasped her hands. "You must hate me."

"No, I don't. I'd have done the same if someone had invaded Cloven Hoof and started laying down the law." I glanced at Dazielle and arched an eyebrow.

"You've got what you wanted," Dazielle said to Suki. "Tempest will sit with you while we do the interview. You agreed you would talk, providing she is here."

Suki gulped in air and nodded. "I'll talk."

I took a step back as Suki's panic flooded the room. No matter how shallowly I breathed, it overwhelmed me. If there was one thing Frank loved, it was a bit of unadulterated, uncontrolled panic. His hot energy curled around my spine in a sticky swirl.

Dazielle stared at me, and her eyes narrowed. "Is everything okay with you?"

"Not really." I gestured for Suki to sit. "Just give me a second." Frank kicked inside me, feeding off the panic in the room.

Dazielle continued to study me, suspicion in her eyes as she fanned a hand in front of her face. "It's really warm in here."

That was Frank's fault. I slid my tongue over my dry teeth. I had to get a grip on him, or this could get messy.

Suki peered at me. "Tempest, you look like you have a fever. You're glowing."

"I can't do this." I backed away from the table and bumped into Dazielle, who'd moved to block the door.

Her hand gripped my shoulder. "You have to. It's the only way we can get Suki to talk."

"You don't understand. I need to get out of here."

Frank's laugh echoed inside my head. "This should be fun, making friends in a building full of angels," he whispered.

"We're not having fun with any angels." I pivoted around and tried to duck past Dazielle, but she stepped into my path.

"Do your job," she said to me.

I resisted the urge to thump her. How could she not sense the problem? Frank's energy prickled up the back of my neck. I was so close to losing control.

"I must get out." My fingers clawed at the handle of the door as Frank continued to slide through me, gaining in strength with every second I was trapped in this room with a panicked wood nymph.

Dazielle finally seemed to twig what was going on. She shoved me backward and pointed a finger at me. "Stay right there." She moved so fast I didn't see her leave the room.

"Tempest, what's wrong?" Suki whispered.

I raised a hand but couldn't speak as an enormous unwelcome burp threatened to come out as Frank inched his control over me.

Dazielle reappeared with the same dizzying amount of speed she'd used to leave the room. She shoved a stale doughnut in my mouth. "Eat."

I tried to spit out the doughnut. Dazielle held on tight and rammed it farther into my mouth. "Eat the doughnut and drink this coffee." She lifted a huge mug of black coffee. "There's plenty of sugar in it. It will help you get your control back."

A flicker of surprise ran through me as I stopped resisting and swallowed the doughnut. I didn't know Dazielle cared enough to help me with my demon issues. Maybe it was just that she wanted to ensure Angel Force wasn't blown apart when Frank came out to play. Whatever her motives, I didn't care. Sugar always calmed Frank, and it was working this time, even though the doughnut was past its best.

"Feeling better?" Dazielle asked as I swallowed the last of the doughnut, grabbed the mug of coffee, and took a huge drink.

"Getting there." Frank had been temporarily placated by the doughnut, and Suki's panic had receded enough that it no longer filled the room and made me twitchy.

I glanced at Suki to see a puzzled look on her face. Maybe she didn't know about Frank. It was probably best if she didn't.

I wiped sugar from my lips and drank more coffee. "Let's do this interview. The sooner it's over, the sooner Suki can go home."

Dazielle stared at me hard before giving a quick nod. The three of us settled at the table. I sat next to

Suki, and Dazielle sat on the other side.

"Tell me what you saw the night Nick was murdered," Dazielle asked Suki.

She glanced at me, and I nodded. "Well, it was dark and late. Almost everyone had gone home from the celebration."

"But not Nick?"

Suki shook her head. "He came back with a camera. He was looking around the stones and taking pictures. I could hear him muttering to himself, but I couldn't hear what he said. I stayed in the forest, so he wouldn't see me."

"You weren't that well-concealed," I said. "Several people spotted you during solstice celebrations."

Suki ducked her head. "I got curious. I love solstice."

"What did you do when you saw Nick?"

"Nothing bad." Suki blinked rapidly, and I felt her panic step up. "I wanted to know what he was interested in. I needed to make sure he wouldn't harm the forest. He was digging small holes around the stones as if looking for something he might have dropped."

"Did he find what he was looking for?"

"Not that I know of."

"How long was Nick there?"

"At least twenty minutes. I'd convinced myself he was nothing to worry about when someone ran out from the shadow of a standing stone. They were dressed in black and had a hood covering their head.

They held a rock in their hand. They hit Nick with it, and he went down."

Dazielle nodded slowly. "Why didn't you come forward with this information as soon as you knew what was going on?"

"I was scared this would happen." Suki gestured around the room. "I couldn't risk being taken from the forest and didn't want my home discovered. It's not that far from the stones, and the thought of all those non-magicals lurking around is horrifying. What if they'd discovered where I live? I'd have to move, and it's taken me years to get it how I want it."

"Are you aware that withholding evidence is a crime?" Dazielle said.

"I hoped you'd figure it out without me," Suki said.

"You have a violent temper," Dazielle said. "I'm going to have two angels off work for days because you can't control your temper."

Suki ducked her head. "I am sorry. I didn't mean to attack anybody. It's one of the reasons I stay out of the way. My temper can get the better of me, and I'd hate for anyone to be injured." She looked at her large brown hands before tucking them onto her lap. "I don't know my own strength."

"You're unusually strong for a wood nymph," Dazielle said.

"That's another reason I stay out of the way. Some people think unusual is wrong."

"We don't, do we?" I looked pointedly at Dazielle. "You shouldn't have to hide if you don't want to."

Suki smiled at me gratefully. "I appreciate that. It's easier for everyone this way. But I promise I had nothing to do with Nick being killed. I was shocked when I saw what happened."

"Okay, let's go back a step. You saw this person hit Nick over the head, and he went down. Did they only hit him once?"

Suki grimaced and shook her head. "Several times. I don't think they knocked him out the first time. They hit him three times. It was horrible."

"Then what?"

"I panicked and ran away. I didn't want them seeing me."

"You didn't see how they moved Nick's body?"

"No, but I didn't go far before I realized I was being a coward. I doubled back and crept to the tree line. By the time I got there, the body was gone. Maybe they used magic to move him."

"Which would make the killer a resident of Willow Tree Falls." Dazielle looked at me. "Maybe I should get your aunt back in for questioning."

"Best if you don't. It's going to be a long time before she forgives you for thinking she killed Nick."

Dazielle shrugged. "Did you see anything else?" she asked Suki.

She nodded. "I went to the stones. I saw where Nick had fallen. I could tell he'd been badly injured by the amount of blood on the ground."

"Hold on. You told me the blood had been covered by the killer, and you didn't see anything when you looked around," I said.

Suki tugged on her bottom lip. "It was me. I covered it. I didn't want the stones to be turned into a circus when everyone else found out. I figured the killer had moved the body and Nick would be found, anyway."

"You corrupted a crime scene." Dazielle sighed and sat back in her seat. "If you're not involved, anyone would think you're best friends with the killer the way you're acting. Not only did you fail to report seeing the murder take place, but you also destroyed evidence."

Suki's eyes filled with tears. "It was wrong. I know that. I am sorry."

"Sorry is not enough," Dazielle said. "I'm going to have to charge you."

"Not with murder," I said.

"A murder charge is still a possibility. We only have Suki's word to go on that this mystery person dressed in black exists. At the very least, she will be charged with assault on my angels, concealing information, and hampering an investigation."

As I was about to protest Suki's innocence, there was a knock on the door. Sablo opened it and looked in the room.

"What is it?" Dazielle asked.

"Another one of those journalists has been attacked."

"Is it James?" I jumped from my seat.

"No, it's a young woman. It was quite some fight she got into."

Dazielle also stood. "This could be connected to Nick. We'll have to continue this interview later."

Suki looked hopeful. "Can I go?"

"Not yet," Dazielle said. "We'll sort you some breakfast and finish the questions later."

Suki slumped in her seat, tears threatening to fall.

"Where did the fight take place?" I asked Sablo.

"At the stone circle."

"Let's get over there," I said.

Dazielle glared at me but nodded. "Okay but stay out of trouble."

"Of course," I said.

Suki caught hold of my hand before I left the room. "There was something else. I heard a strange noise by the stones as I was coming back. It was like a purring sound."

I glanced over my shoulder, keen not to let Dazielle get away. "Like an animal sound?"

"No, more like an engine sound."

"Was it a bike engine, like the kind of thing Rhett drives?"

"I think it was a car. I'm not used to seeing them so close to the stone circle, so the sound surprised me. It might have nothing to do with it, but I won't hide anything else from you. I do want to help sort this out."

"Thanks, it could be useful. When I get a second, I'll look into it."

"Thanks for helping me." Suki let go of my hand. "Are you feeling better?"

I gave her shoulder a brief squeeze. "After a stale doughnut and a coffee, I'm fine. Sit tight. I'll be back to get you out as soon as possible."

I hurried after Dazielle, who had already left the building. The engine sound could be relevant. If the killer had used a vehicle to move Nick, that would narrow down the suspects. Few people drove in Willow Tree Falls. It made it much more likely to be a non-magical involved.

Maybe this new information wouldn't matter if we were about to unmask the killer. If they'd attacked someone else, they must be unstable and taking more risks. Risks led to mistakes. Mistakes that meant I could catch them, solve this murder, and get Suki released.

Chapter 17

Wiggles joined me as I raced out of Angel Force and along the road, catching fleeting glimpses of Dazielle as she soared across the street and up the hill to the stones.

"Where's the fire?" he asked.

"It's not a fire; it's a fight."

"Who's involved?"

"Sablo said it was a woman journalist. I don't think there are any here, at least, none that I've seen. It might be Jenny or maybe Rachel."

As we reached the top of the hill, my mouth dropped open. One of the enormous ancient stones in the stone circle had been knocked over. A large crack ran across its center. It looked like an ancient fallen warrior. The stones had been here for thousands of years, always steadfast, never at risk of collapse. How could this have happened?

"Someone did not like that stone." Wiggles trotted over and sniffed around it. "Who has the power to take down one of these?"

"I'm not sure I want to find out." Three angels were inside the stone circle, surrounding someone who was sprawled on the ground.

I cast a worried look at the broken stone before hurrying over to see who it was.

Dazielle glanced at me and nodded. "It's Jenny. She's out cold."

I peered around Dazielle and saw Jenny on her back. A large red mark marred one cheek, and her hands were bleeding.

"It looks like she's been clawed by an animal." I looked closely at her hands. They were laced with deep scratches.

"It wasn't an animal. Someone reported seeing two women fighting inside the stones," Dazielle said.

"Who was the other woman?"

"That's what we need to find out as soon as Jenny wakes up."

A shudder of cold ran up my spine. Something felt horribly off here. You did not knock over an ancient, powerful stone full of magic without having significant abilities.

I stepped away from the angels as they made preparations to move Jenny and took a slow walk around the inside of the circle. The whole time I did, Frank pulsed through me. It was as if he could sense the dark power and was not happy.

Wiggles strode along beside me, his hackles up and his eyes glowing. He could also sense the weird vibes the place gave off.

Dark magic had been involved in this fight, and its foul essence still lingered like a silent fart in an elevator.

I made it halfway around the stones before Dazielle joined me, her expression grim. "You sense it, don't you?"

"Something is off, here. I'm getting this weird tingle and not in a good way."

She nodded, and her eyes tightened. "I bet your demon does, as well. It takes like to know like."

I nodded and looked regretfully at the stone. I didn't know how we'd repair the damage.

"Whoever or whatever has that dark power, we need to stop it," Dazielle said. "I don't know how Jenny is involved with this, but if she's come into contact with dark magic, it could have harmed her. It's hard to predict how non-magicals will react when they come face-to-face with the truth about magic."

"It looks like she didn't come off too well," I said.

"We'll get her to the hospital for a thorough check-up. Only then will we know how badly she's been affected and how long-lasting the impact will be."

We both turned as a scream rang out. Jenny was sitting bolt upright, one hand raised, pointing back toward Willow Tree Falls.

I ran over with Dazielle as Jenny slumped back on the ground.

"What happened?" Dazielle looked at the angels surrounding Jenny. "Did she say anything?"

"She said the name Rachel," one of the angels said.

"That was Nick's girlfriend," Dazielle said.

I stared at Jenny. It seemed a little on the dramatic side to sit upright, scream another person's name, and collapse. Was she trying to tell us that Rachel was the other woman involved in the fight?

We waited a moment to see if Jenny would say anything else, but she was out cold again.

I walked back to the broken stone and placed my hand on top of it. "Don't worry. We'll find out who did this to you. I wish you could talk and tell us what happened."

Wiggles sniffed around the stone. "We should leave."

"Are you sensing something bad?"

"I know you never like to run away from a fight, but even I might think twice about going up against anyone who can bring down a standing stone." Wiggles sniffed the stone and backed up a few steps.

"My hellhound is scared? You're supposed to be fearless." I tried to make light of the situation, but it was hard to do so when my own nerves bounced with a warning.

Wiggles sniffed around some more. "I'm just saying I like our lives as they are. I don't mind a bit of investigating now and again, but neither of us will be able to do that if whatever knocked over this stone comes after us."

"You don't think I can handle them?"

Wiggles' ears pricked. "Maybe Frank could."

"Let's not try that experiment. For all we know, Frank, and whoever did this, could be best buddies. If I let him out to go on the hunt, all that will do is release another dangerous power into Willow Tree Falls."

"I'm just saying maybe Frank can be an asset for once."

I wasn't convinced, but Frank did have a remarkable lack of morals and fear. He would do anything to win.

"Tempest, you might as well go home." Dazielle walked over. "We can't question Jenny at the moment. I've put out a call to find Rachel and see what she knows about this fight. Right now, I'm at a loss to figure out what happened."

"Fair enough." For once, I was glad Dazielle was getting rid of me. "I'll keep an eye out for Rachel."

"Be careful around her. If she got Jenny in this state, she's not safe to be around."

"I'll give her a wide berth if I see her." I headed back down the hill and along the main street with Wiggles. One stale doughnut and a mug of coffee would not suffice for breakfast. I headed to Tilly's for a much-needed fix of food and a chance to think about this fight and what it meant, if anything, in Nick's murder.

Tilly hurried over when she saw me settle at a table. "You look... like you've had a busy night."

"You won't believe the half of it." I gave her a quick update about what had happened to Suki and my unenjoyable evening at Angel Force.

Tilly sat at the table with a mug of herbal tea, her eyes growing wider as I finished the story.

"That's such a terrible thing to do to Suki. Are they going to let her out? The angels aren't continuing this ridiculous line of questioning, are they?"

I looked at her and narrowed my eyes. "That depends on if the actual killer comes forward anytime soon. Is there anything you'd like to tell me about that night you spent with Nick?"

Tilly's cheeks flushed. "You might as well know, and to be clear, it wasn't the whole night. I only kept quiet about it because I was embarrassed."

"What do you have to be embarrassed about? You did kiss Nick?"

Tilly looked up at the ceiling as if seeking inspiration. "Okay, I did think he was cute. I can't explain it, but I think a lot of non-magicals are gorgeous. He came in the first day he arrived, being charming. He had that lovely accent, and he smelt so good."

I wrinkled my nose. "He didn't smell that great."

"Nick smelt like a garden full of spicy flowers. It made me want to wrap myself around him and snuggle him tight."

"You have the strangest taste in men. So, what happened the night you were seen together?"

She stroked a finger around the rim of her mug. "I might have invited him here for dinner."

"You asked him on a date?"

"Sort of. I played it down, but he was happy enough to get the invitation. He was also happy enough to make out with me."

"Hold on. In what order did this happen? He accepted your date and came to dinner. Then did you make out and eat or eat and make out, or did you do both?"

"A little of both. Nick was very friendly. I didn't know about his girlfriend. I had seen a woman hanging around him a lot. I didn't look into it; ignorance is bliss and all that, but I assumed it might have been his assistant."

I arched an eyebrow. "How convenient not to inquire if Nick had a girlfriend before kissing him."

"Hey, I'm the innocent party here. Nick knew he was involved with Rachel and decided to forget about it when our lips locked. He's the one who cheated."

"Okay, so you had a make-out session and then served him dinner?"

"Yes, I thought it was going so well. It was busy here that night, but I'd saved him a special table, one by the counter so I could join him as much as possible. He had his starter, which he loved. Then I served him my speciality ale and tarragon pie. You know the one with the crispy puff pastry top and rich sauce?"

"Of course, I love your pies."

"Exactly, everybody loves my pies. No one has ever complained about my pies."

I tilted my head. "Until Nick?"

Tilly nodded sagely. "Until Nick. I was telling the truth about him complaining about my food. He left half the pie. I jokingly asked if there was something wrong with it. I expected him to say it was fabulous, but he was too full or was saving room for dessert. No, do you know what he said?"

"Nothing good about your pie?"

"He said it wasn't his sort of thing. I was disappointed but decided not to push him. We had a glass of wine together, and I gently prodded about the food to make sure he wasn't unhappy. He brushed it away and made out like it wasn't anything important, but I knew something was wrong."

"I'm guessing it was important to you? More important than impressing a hot non-magical?"

"Of course. This is my pie on the line. More than that, it's my restaurant on the line. If word gets out that people aren't finishing their food, it will look bad on me."

"One unfinished pie will not ruin you."

"It's a slippery slope to bankruptcy and empty tables," Tilly said. "Anyway, I walked him out of the restaurant, and we had a friendly smooch good night. That's when I got him to admit it."

"What did he admit?"

"Nick said my pie had a soggy bottom. Can you imagine it! I've never cooked a pie with a soggy bottom in my life. My bottom is always perfection."

"You do lovely bottoms," I said.

"And that was it, no more kissing with Nick. I was devastated. I'd wasted the whole evening on a guy who was not only cheating on his girlfriend but thought my pies were substandard."

"Does that mean you're no longer interested in non-magicals?"

"I won't be interested if they're going to be rude about my bottoms." Tilly took a sip of herbal tea and leaned closer. "And that's not the only thing. Nick's conversation was boring. He kept going on about this ring he wanted to find."

I sat up in my seat. "The Ring of Halo?"

"He didn't give it a name." Tilly's eyes widened. "That's not what he was looking for, was it? He can't have thought it was a good idea to dig up that nasty piece of magic."

"Most likely he did. The ring has gone missing. Nick sounds like he was obsessed with it. I'm reckoning that's what got him killed."

Tilly drummed her fingers on the table. "I have terrible taste in men. They hate my food and are trying to use dark magic items they should have no business knowing anything about. He was so cute, though."

"No, he wasn't. You do have terrible taste in non-magical men."

"Oh, come off it. Even you have to admit Nick was cute."

"He was too floppy-haired for my liking. I like my men a bit—"

"Rough around the edges? Stubbled and sitting astride an enormous motorbike? The leader of a certain biker gang?" Tilly waggled her brows at me and grinned.

I swatted Tilly's hand. "Enough of that. This information still makes you a suspect. You could be seen as romantically involved with Nick, and he insulted you. How far would you go to keep your soggy bottom a secret?" I wasn't being serious, but the horrified look on Tilly's face was worth it.

"I hated him for not loving my pies, but I wouldn't kill him for it. My plan was to make a special pie and leave it for Nick. He'd know then my pies are lovely. It's just a shame I never got the chance."

"Your soggy bottom secret will go to the grave."

"It was a soggy bottomed lie!" She smiled at me. "You don't seriously think I'm involved, do you?"

"No, and the more I learn about this, the more I'm convinced it's one of the non-magicals. In fact, after this fight Jenny was in, it could be Rachel."

"The jealous girlfriend, who lied about a pregnancy and seems more interested in her social climbing than finding true love. She sounds like the perfect killer." Tilly stood from the table. "I'd better get on. Let me know how things go."

I grabbed a couple of filled baguettes to go and left Tilly to her work. I was glad she'd finally come clean about her involvement with Nick. I'd never taken her seriously as a suspect, but Dazielle would only start hounding her if she got desperate enough and the real killer wasn't found quickly.

But our chat hadn't helped me figure out what had gone on between Jenny and Rachel at the standing stones. I had to get to the hospital and see if Jenny had regained consciousness, so I could find out who she was fighting with and what the fight was about.

Chapter 18

"Play charades with me." Wiggles nudged me with his nose.

"We're in a hospital waiting room. It's not a place to play games." I dropped the dog-eared magazine I'd been reading.

"How about name that tune? I'll bark a tune, and you guess what it is."

"No barking. You'll upset the patients. I snuck you in here without anyone seeing. If a nurse discovers you, you'll be kicked out." I had to admit I was as bored as Wiggles. We'd been waiting for three hours to get news on Jenny. So far, she'd done nothing other than mutter in her sleep and twitch a lot.

The door to the waiting room opened, and Dazielle walked in.

I jumped up from my seat. "Any news?"

"Jenny has regained consciousness. She keeps saying Rachel's name over and over again. She said

Rachel was like a crazy person, her eyes were gleaming and she was foaming at the mouth before she attacked her."

"Rachel sounds like she's had a bite from a rabid dog."

"She sounds possessed. You don't have any demons unaccounted for from the prison who might have gotten to Rachel, do you?"

I scowled at Dazielle. "You're not pinning this on my family letting a demon go. The prison is locked tight, same as always."

Dazielle nodded. "I figured as much, but it would have been an easy explanation."

"What now?"

"Jenny's awake if you want to talk to her," Dazielle said. "Keep it brief and no stressing her out. She keeps falling asleep and is sedated, so she might not make much sense."

I left Wiggles in the waiting room and headed out with Dazielle along the clean white hospital corridor. We walked into a small private room. Jenny lay in the bed, her hands bandaged.

She looked at me and a small smile crossed her face. "Hi, Tempest. It's nice of you to come to see me."

"Sorry to say, it's on official business." I glanced at Dazielle, and she nodded. "We're hoping you can help us shed light on what happened between you and Rachel in the stone circle."

Her smile vanished, and a worried look entered her eyes. "I wish I knew. She was so scary. She kept lunging and scratching me. Her nails felt more like claws every time they made contact. My hands will be sore for weeks."

"Why did she attack you?" I asked.

Jenny chewed on her bottom lip. "She was jealous of me."

"Of what in particular?"

"I had a good relationship with Nick. Rachel is suspicious of anyone who spent time with Nick. She was insecure about their relationship. And she lied about it, as well. Do you remember the night Nick died, and Rachel said she was his fiancée?"

I nodded. "Sure. I also remember how surprised you looked when she revealed that."

"Because it wasn't true. Nick never asked Rachel to marry him. He never would."

"Are you suggesting you and Nick had a romantic connection?"

"No, nothing romantic. I saw him more as a big brother, a sort of mentor. He might have had a little crush on me, but I liked to keep things professional. We worked well together and were talking about partnering up when he got his staff position at the paper. It was a professional relationship but with the bonus of us being friends. It made Rachel's blood boil. She was always making snide comments and ordering me around like I was her assistant. That was the only thing that annoyed me about Nick. He never stood up to her. He let Rachel walk all over him just for a quiet life."

"That must have annoyed you," I said.

"It did. I mentioned it a few times, but Nick said he was dealing with it, and Rachel wouldn't be around for much longer."

"He was planning to ditch her?"

"I think so. Maybe that's what tipped her over the edge. Rachel was so clingy and annoying. Nick had had enough. He wanted out."

"Rachel wanted you both dead because of that?" Dazielle asked. "She killed Nick because he rejected her and decided to get even with you because she was jealous of your friendship with Nick?"

"It's the only reason I can think of for her to attack me so savagely," Jenny said.

"What about the broken stone?" I asked. "What do you know about that?"

"A broken stone?" Confusion crossed Jenny's face.

"Yes, the ancient hunk of rock that has stood in the same spot for thousands of years and got ripped out of the ground when you fought with Rachel." I glanced at Dazielle and raised my eyebrows.

"Oh, it was already like that," Jenny said. "When I got there, the stone had fallen on its side. I figured it must have been done during the celebration. It's an old stone, so it could have crumbled when people jumped on it."

That couldn't be true. Those stones withstood anything. "What were you doing at the stone circle?"

"Getting a few last shots. It was something Nick taught me to do. Always get more footage than you think you'll need. It can come in handy during editing. I was going to splice it together when I got back to work."

"And Rachel just happened to find you there?"

"I guess so," Jenny said. "I can't figure out why she's still hanging around. There's no reason for her to be here now Nick has gone."

"I told her to stay," I said. "I'm glad I did if she's involved with this attack on you, as well."

Dazielle's pocket vibrated. She pulled out a small flat version of a snow globe and turned away discreetly to look at the message. To a non-magical, it would look like she was checking her mobile.

She shoved it back in her pocket and turned to the bed. "Rachel has been spotted."

Jenny sat up in the bed, bright dots of color appearing on her cheeks. "I must see her."

"You need to stay where you are," Dazielle said. "You've had a shock and are in no condition to leave the hospital."

"I have to know where she is and what she's up to," Jenny demanded. "She tried to kill me."

"We'll get the answers you need." Dazielle looked at me. "She's apparently being... difficult. The others could do with a hand."

I interpreted difficult as out of control crazy because she was using magic she couldn't control. I nodded at Dazielle. "Let's go."

"Wait! What about me? I need to come with you." Jenny struggled to the edge of the bed, flipping up and down because she couldn't use her hands to balance herself.

Dazielle touched her shoulder. "Stay here. We'll keep you up to date. I'll post an angel outside the hospital, so you don't need to worry about your safety. Rachel can't get to you in here."

Jenny's lips pressed together. She nodded and slid down the bed. "Okay, I guess I feel better. Make sure you get Rachel, though. She's evil."

"What do you think of her story?" Dazielle asked as we hurried along the corridor toward the exit.

I ducked my head into the waiting room and whistled for Wiggles to join us. "I believe Rachel is the jealous type, but to kill Jenny because she had a good working relationship with Nick doesn't seem right. This has to do with that ring Nick was after."

"You think Rachel has this ring? That's why she's acting out of character?"

As we stepped out of the hospital, the air was thick with an unhealthy throb of murky feeling magic. "That's what we're about to find out."

"Rachel was last seen outside Mystic Mushroom. I'll meet you there." Dazielle took flight and soared along the street on her enormous white wings.

"Come on, Wiggles." I raced after Dazielle.

"This place has a bad vibe to it," Wiggles said. "It smells like three-day-old barbecue meat that's been re-heated and covered in sauce to hide the rot."

I grimaced. The place did feel out of sync with its normal healthy brew of magic. The feeling of dense, sticky dark magic grew stronger as we neared the main street.

"What's the plan?" Wiggles asked.

"Find Rachel and take her down if she's got her hands on magic she can't control."

"Simple but effective."

The closer I got to the dark magic, the more Frank twitched and pulsed inside me.

"Not now," I said to him.

"You're going to need me for this one," he whispered.

"I can handle this."

"Let me handle it for you," Frank said. "I have met this power before. It's more than one little witch can handle."

"Stay down. I don't trust you."

"Right now, you have no choice."

I lurched to the side, stumbling over my own feet as Frank's energy zoomed up my spine and prickled on the back of my neck.

I gritted my teeth and focused on keeping him under my control. He could not get out, not now. Dark magic twitched all around us, only encouraging Frank's energy to pulse harder through me, making my heart pound and sweat trickle down my back.

Wiggles whined and nudged my hand. His eyes showed concern. "Do you need help?"

"Get out of here. I'm not safe to be around. Frank wants to come out to play."

"Shall I get anyone?"

"Just stay back. You can't be caught up in this."

Wiggles was a tough hellhound, but if he got caught in the middle of a fight between Frank and this dark energy tainting Willow Tree Falls, he might not come out looking too good.

He whined a couple more times but knew better than to be too close to me when Frank took over.

I breathed a sigh of relief as I saw him turn and race along the street. I couldn't be sure, but it looked like he was heading to Mom's house. He'd better not bring the family into this. I couldn't risk any of them getting hurt when Frank emerged.

I sucked in a deep breath, knowing I was losing the fight. "Do not kill anyone," I said to him.

"Not even the dark power that is making the whole of Willow Tree Falls quake?"

"It can be contained."

"We'll see about that." His energy smothered me from head to toe. A gross tasting sulfurous belch shot from my lips as Frank gained full control of my body.

The world took on its usual red tint as Frank surveyed the surroundings. I strode along the street, heading toward Mystic Mushroom and the growing crowd of white clad angels.

Dazielle's head shot up as I approached. She gestured the other angels back. "Take your positions. Focus on keeping everyone else safe." She backed away as I neared. "Tempest, I can't help you this time."

"I need no help from an angel," Frank said. I willed him to slow down and not attack Dazielle. She was not a threat to us.

But Frank had no interest in the angels. He looked over Dazielle's shoulder at the wild-haired woman standing in the middle of the street. Her shoulders were hunched, and she was missing a shoe.

Even though Frank was in control, I felt shocked when I saw the state Rachel was in. It wasn't the state of her clothing that was alarming. On her right hand sat a glowing purple ring.

"Tempest, be careful," Dazielle warned. "Rachel has already taken out two angels."

I heard her but couldn't respond.

Frank made a dismissive gesture at Dazielle as he strode past and stood facing Rachel. "We meet again."

Rachel's head rose slowly. Her eyes were a dense swirling black. "I thought I smelled something sour, a traitorous demon."

"What is controlling Rachel?" I asked Frank.

"Her name is Eligos."

My fear only made Frank stronger. "Isn't Eligos male?"

"She can be. I prefer her in her female form."

"Your preferences are of no interest to me," Eligos said.

"It has not always been that way," Frank said.

"It is since you've been schooled by a witch." Rachel's mouth moved, but the voice coming out of her was anything but human.

Frank hissed and advanced on Eligos. My body heated to an uncomfortable level, and my clothes were soaked with sweat.

"Be careful," I cautioned Frank. "You're fighting in a human body. My body. I need it in one piece."

"I make no guarantees."

Perfect. Frank was in full-on hunter mode, and I could do nothing but watch from the sidelines as he trashed my body.

I caught a glimpse of Dazielle, who was focused on crowd control and keeping any non-magicals from seeing what was about to go down between two demons.

Eligos crouched and charged Frank, who dodged me out of the way with ease. My fist made contact with the back of Rachel's head, and my knuckles protested as they slammed into bone.

"Go easy!" I yelped.

Frank simply laughed as he threw himself onto Rachel's back. This was fun to him, but if he didn't rein it in, I'd be wearing bruises for weeks.

"Magic barrier in place," Dazielle shouted to me.

That barrier would do nothing to protect me but would stop the gawking non-magical onlookers from seeing the truth about Willow Tree Falls. They weren't going to tick *watched two demons in a knock-down fight* off their bucket lists today.

Eligos flipped me on the ground. I just had time to roll out the way of Rachel's bare foot as she tried to smoosh my face into the dirt. Death by calloused heel was not the way to go.

"We need to get that ring off her finger," I said to Frank.

"It would look lovely in my collection." Frank pushed me to my feet, and the demons circled each other.

"We're not keeping it." Once I had that ring, it was going somewhere no one could get their hands on it.

Rachel grabbed me in a headlock, and we hit the ground again. Her arm wrapped around my neck, and she squeezed so tightly my eyes bulged. That ring was giving her serious amounts of muscle power.

"Frank! Do something." Only Frank could hear my plea, and I had to be desperate to ask him for anything, but if he didn't get me out of this headlock, something was going to break.

"I'm having a little trouble." I'd never heard Frank sound so panicked. "Need a way out."

"Tempest, hold on. We're here."

I recognized Aurora's voice. Through my tear-filled eyes, I spotted Aurora, Mom, Auntie Queenie, and Granny Dottie standing in a row. I just had time to shut my eyes as their combined magic blasted into Rachel and Eligos.

Rachel's body slammed to the ground, taking me with her. Fortunately, her iron tight grip loosened. I shoved myself out from under her arm.

Frank took control again. He grabbed the finger that had the Ring of Halo on it and tugged. The sickening crack I heard was bone breaking. The ring slid into my hand, and I rolled away as angels piled on top of Rachel.

Frank was still on fire inside me, and he wasn't done fighting just yet. For a second, I had control of my own voice.

"Hit me!" I yelled at my family.

Aurora's eyes widened. "Are you sure?"

"Blast me with something powerful." My control was gone as Frank's energy shot up my spine and over my head.

A warm blast of magic flowed through me, and I relaxed. I knew this power. It was a feeling I'd grown up surrounded by. It was love and protection and kindness. It was everything my family stood for. It gave me enough of a boost to shove away Frank's power and regain control.

I rolled over and slammed face first into the side of a building.

Frank still lingered below the surface, but he wasn't pushing me. If I didn't know any better, I'd think he was concerned about my well-being or maybe simply licking a wound or two of his own.

I lay there, watching the flurry of white feathers as angels subdued Rachel. She was still holding residual power from the ring I had yanked off her finger but looked easier to control.

The angels pulled her onto her feet, her hands behind her back, and marched her away.

Dazielle walked over to me, caution etched on her face. "How are you doing?"

I coughed, and a sulphurous belch came out. I waved my hand in front of my face. "I'm still not quite myself."

Dazielle held out a hand to help me up, but I gestured her away. "I think I'll stay here for a while and make sure everything is as it should be."

Dazielle nodded. "You've just saved Willow Tree Falls."

"Does that mean you owe me one?"

Dazielle snorted in surprise then nodded. "Perhaps it does."

I watched as she strolled away, confidence oozing from her now she had success in bringing Rachel to justice.

Wiggles bounded over, followed by Mom, Aurora, Auntie Queenie, and Granny Dottie.

I forced myself to stand, despite not trusting my knees to hold me up. Wiggles paced in front of me. He looked anything but the chilled-out hellhound he usually was.

Mom engulfed me in a hug. "How are you? I hope our magic didn't do you harm."

"You know me. I come from tough stock." I stepped back and smiled at everyone. "Thanks for the blast of magic."

Granny Dottie also hugged me. "We were worried about you, my girl."

"There's nothing to worry about. Not anymore." I opened my hand to reveal the ring.

Everyone took a step back, their eyes wide as they stared at it.

"Do you know what you're holding?" Mom asked.

"The reason everything's been so weird around here lately."

"You must get rid of it," Granny Dottie said.

"I brought this to contain it." Auntie Queenie opened what looked like an ordinary wooden box.

As I slid the ring inside, it glowed a dazzling purple as she snapped the lid on it. "That will keep it safe for a short while."

"It needs to go back to the forest. Suki is its protector," I said.

"We'll make sure no one else gets their hands on it," Mom said.

"That sounds good to me." I felt my eyes trying to close. Having a fight with a human possessed by a demon was never my idea of fun.

Aurora looped an arm around my waist. "Let's get you home."

I smiled feebly as I let them lead me away. Home, a week of sleep, and no more hassle sounded just about perfect to me.

Chapter 19

After several hearty meals fed to me by Mom and an amazing night's rest in my old bedroom at the family home, I felt a hundred times better. Willow Tree Falls was safe again, the Ring of Halo had been contained, and it looked like Rachel was neck deep in Nick's murder. She must have killed him to get her hands on the ring. All the angels had to do was get a confession out of her. Even they couldn't mess that up. Everything felt right with the world.

I walked down the stairs and into the kitchen. Mom was in her usual place by the stove, stirring what smelled like an enormous vat of strawberry preserve.

"Would you like some breakfast?" she asked.

"Actually, I thought I'd go out and celebrate after yesterday's fun," I said.

"My food isn't good enough to celebrate over?"

I gave her a quick kiss on the cheek. As much as I loved my mom, she could be a little on the stifling side. I was used to living with just Wiggles and not being fussed over. "Thanks, but I'll pass. I've got a couple of loose ends to tie up with this case. I need to report in to Angel Force to make sure Suki has been released and Rachel is safely behind bars with no chance of getting out."

"Of course. Do tell Suki she's welcome at ours anytime. We always have room for a wood nymph."

After saying goodbye, I left with Wiggles and strolled back to the main street.

"Can we have pizza for breakfast?" Wiggles asked.

"I was thinking an enormous smoothie bowl covered in nuts, grated chocolate, and dried fruit."

"What's wrong with pizza?"

"It's not exactly a health food. I feel like I need to take better care of myself after yesterday." I touched a bruise on my butt. Everything felt a little sore, even after Mom had performed several healing spells on me.

"You might, but I'm still stress eating after seeing you almost killed by a demon."

"You're stress eating?" I rolled my eyes. "We'll consider pizza for lunch."

A white van was parked outside of Unicorn's Trough as we neared it. James was strutting around the outside of the van, a smug look on his face.

He scowled when he saw me before glaring at Wiggles and being careful to keep a safe distance. "I don't suppose I can get an exclusive story on what happened here yesterday? I've been asking around, and everyone is tight-lipped. That always means there's something juicy if they don't want to tell me."

"I have no clue what you're talking about."

"I have a source who tells me you were in the center of the action," James said. "It will be a real scoop if I can find out what it was, especially since I have my new promotion. I need to make a splash with an exclusive."

"I'm happy for you. I still don't know what I can do to help."

"You can tell me if my source is correct."

I glanced around, wondering exactly who his source was. As soon as I discovered them, I'd make sure they never talked to another journalist again. "What do you think you know?"

James grinned. "There's something different about you. You might be the next Uri Geller."

I arched an eyebrow. "Isn't that the guy who bends spoons?"

"He's psychic. Some believe he has magic powers."

I snorted a laugh. "We've been here before. A smart guy like you believes in magic?"

"I'm not the only one. My source tells me that the hunt for magic is what got Nick killed. My source also tells me Rachel went off the rails and killed him for it."

"If that's true, then magic doesn't sound like the sort of thing you want to mess with. You need to look for another story. How about a sympathetic report of your good friend Nick Saunders?"

"That's boring. I'm not leaving here until I get the truth about you and this place. There's more to this backward little hamlet than hot water that stinks and ancient stones. You're hiding something here."

My nails dug into my palms as I smiled at him. "Why don't you come have breakfast with me? I'd like to hear everything you know." Then I could make a decision about what to do with James. I couldn't risk him leaving Willow Tree Falls and running a lurid story about us. We'd get all kinds of spook hunters arriving to see the freaks of the village if I did.

James winked at me and adjusted his collar. "I knew you wouldn't be able to resist me for long."

"You don't know what a struggle it's been. This way." I headed into Unicorn's Trough and nodded at Brogan as I sat at my favorite table by the window.

James settled opposite me and stretched his legs. "I have to admit I wasn't looking forward to yet another boring small town story, but being here has been an adventure."

"You don't say. What kind of adventure have you been having?"

"This place is full of secrets. Everyone who lives here is hiding something. I believe it's the same something."

"You don't really believe the magic theory, do you?"

Brogan came over, a curious look on his face as he saw me with James, especially since we'd argued the last time we were in here. "What will it be, folks?"

"I'll have the goddess smoothie bowl and the biggest mug of coffee you can find," I said.

James ordered waffles and fresh fruit. "What is this big mystery? I thought it might be you were all hiding an old diamond mine or an untapped source of oil and didn't want anybody to know about it."

"No, it's nothing like that. This place is as dull as you think it is."

"There is no magic ring?" He raised his eyebrows and stared hard at me.

"Nick did talk about a ring," I said. "Maybe he meant an engagement ring for his unstable girlfriend."

"It has to be more than that." James drummed his fingers on the table in an irritating rhythm. "The police won't tell me anything."

"That's because there's nothing to tell. It's time for you to move on and hassle another village for a story that doesn't exist."

He watched me in silence, his gaze full of mistrust. I was telling him nothing. It was time to change the subject.

"Do you know how Jenny's doing?" I asked.

"Why should I be interested in her?"

I gave a small shake of my head. "She's your assistant."

James shrugged. "She's out of the hospital. I've got her loading up the van."

This guy was a real piece of work. "You do know she was attacked yesterday by Rachel, right?"

"Sure, but there's nothing wrong with her now."

That was strange. Jenny couldn't even sit up in bed unaided when I saw her. "Her hands were messed up. She shouldn't be carrying anything and definitely not loading your equipment into a van."

"She said it wasn't a problem. Jenny had some bandage straps on her hands, but I don't see what all the fuss is about. There's barely a scratch on her. She was being hysterical."

"Jenny has a right to be. She was in a bad way when she was found after Rachel attacked her."

"You know what women can be like when they get catty." James smirked at me. "Have you ever fought over a guy?"

"They weren't fighting over a guy."

"That's not what Jenny says. She told me Rachel got jealous and went for her. I can't understand it. Nick had no drive, no get up and go. Why would they have fought over him? Rachel needs a real man if she wants to go places."

"Do you think you're that real man?"

His smug smile turned lecherous. "Why don't you let me show you?"

"There's no need. I've already made my mind up about you."

"What does that pretty little mind of yours tell you?" James leaned over the table and tried to grab my hand.

"Is there a problem here?"

I looked up, surprised to see Axel standing at the counter, glaring at us.

I waved away his concern. "Nothing for you to worry about."

Axel glared at James before turning away.

"Is that your boyfriend?" James asked.

"A friend. So, you really made Jenny go back to work already?"

"Of course, if she stops working, she'll be forgotten in five minutes. There are always people chasing after these assistant positions, looking to get a foot in the door with journalism. She can't afford to take time off."

"She must be in a lot of pain."

"When you're motivated, you get things done," James said. "And I'm motivated to get the truth out of you." He finally succeeded in catching hold of my hand and pulled it across the table toward him.

Instead of yanking my hand away, I gripped hold of his wrist and held on tight, pulsing a spell through my fingers and into his skin. "How about I tell you a story? In Willow Tree Falls, there is a beautiful old thermal spa. That's the true magic of this place. People who go in the thermal spa leave feeling ten years younger and invigorated."

James's eyes glazed over as my magic weaved through his thoughts, removing his desire to tell the truth about the village. He would have his story, but it would be the same boring old story everyone told after they'd visited this place. The magic lay in the thermal spa waters and the ancient stones. That was all there was to it.

Despite wanting to yank my fingers off his clammy skin, I kept hold of James's hand until I was certain my magic had done its job.

Brogan walked over with our food. Concern crossed his face as he sensed my magic. "I hope there's not going to be any trouble here."

I smiled sweetly at him. "There's nothing for you to worry about. James is going to take his food to go, though."

Brogan looked at James, and he nodded. "That's right. I need to go."

Brogan returned a moment later with a bag for James. He wandered out of the cafe looking happy and completely oblivious to the truth.

Brogan eased himself into James's empty seat. "Tempest, you don't need me to tell you to be careful using magic around non-magicals."

I scooped up a big mouthful of smoothie. "He deserved it. He was a jerk, whose only interest is himself and what he can get out of a situation. He knows Willow Tree Falls is different. He wasn't going to stop questioning people until he found out the truth. I can't afford for that to happen. We don't need people poking their nose where it's not wanted. When that happens, dangerous magic gets uncovered, and people get hurt."

Brogan looked out the window at James, who sat on the bumper of his van eating his waffles. "I guess he did deserve it. How are you doing? I saw most of what happened yesterday. You took quite a beating."

"I feel surprisingly good. It was worth getting a few bruises to get this whole mess sorted out." I glanced out the window. Even though everything was resolved, what James had told me about Jenny's quick recovery unsettled me. There was no way she should be using her hands after they'd been so badly injured.

Brogan touched my arm. "What's on your mind?"

"Maybe it's nothing. I need to close down this case and move on. There's bound to be some demon who needs a butt whipping."

"The Ring of Halo is in safe hands, I'm assuming," Brogan said.

"It's secure. I'll be giving it back to Suki as soon as I can. She can keep it safe along with all the other magic in the forest. She's done a great job for so many years. I'm not going to let one slip-up go against her."

"Good. I don't like to think of her alone in the forest. She is welcome here anytime. And until she feels comfortable enough to use the front door, I will keep supplying her with food out the back."

"She's good at taking care of herself, but I know she'll appreciate that." It sounded like Suki would be busy from now on; she was getting so many invitations.

Brogan left me to finish my food alone and headed off to serve other customers.

Once breakfast was out of the way, I walked over to Angel Force's headquarters with Wiggles to find Dazielle in the reception area.

She raised her eyebrows when she saw me. "I didn't expect to see you around for at least a week."

"I'm already feeling much better. How's everything going with Rachel?"

"She's been charged with Nick's murder and the illegal possession of a magic artifact."

"Did she confess to the murder?"

"Not so much. She keeps saying she knows nothing about it, but it has to be her. Maybe she got her hands on the ring after Nick had discovered it and lost control. We both saw how unstable she was when wearing the ring."

"You don't think she's innocent?"

"Not for a second. She might say she is, but I don't believe it."

There was that niggle again in the back of my head, telling me to keep prodding this case. "Is there physical evidence she struck Nick and moved his body?"

Dazielle's eyes narrowed. "Not yet. What are you getting at?"

"I don't know. It might be nothing, and I agree Rachel needs to be charged with handling the artifact, but Nick's murder, I'm not so sure."

"You seemed sure yesterday."

"I was. I mean, I am. It most likely was Rachel. What about Suki? I hope you're dropping all charges."

"We're dropping the murder charge, but we're charging Suki with assault," Dazielle said.

"Come off it. She defended herself against your attack. That's not a crime."

"Suki should have come quietly. We didn't want to hurt her."

"She wasn't to know that. You stalked through her forest, stamping around and terrifying her. She reacted just like any wood nymph would."

"The problem is she's a six-foot wood nymph with arms like tree trunks and a quick temper. Suki lashed out and injured people. She even landed you on your butt. She has to answer for that."

I had a bruise on the back of my head to remind me of that, but I didn't hold it against Suki. "What will happen to her?"

"I've checked her record. It's a first offense, but she could still serve time inside. She would also benefit from a rehabilitation course to learn how to control her temper."

"She can't go to jail. She'll be picked on and miserable. Suki's had enough of that in her life."

"It's no less than she deserves."

"What Suki deserves is to be left alone, so she can look after her forest. We owe a lot to Suki for protecting dangerous magic and keeping us safe from it. She makes one small mistake and gets shoved into jail. That's unfair. If she goes inside, we'll all be vulnerable. You take her out of the forest, and the whole of Willow Tree Falls will be at risk."

Dazielle scowled at me. "What do you suggest we do with her? She's not being let go, or she won't realize she's done anything wrong."

I rubbed my chin as an idea formed. "Suki can serve her sentence with me."

Dazielle's brow wrinkled. "What would she do with you?"

"I'll help her feel more comfortable in her skin. If you like, I'll make sure she goes to her rehabilitation program." This was becoming a habit I wasn't sure I wanted, helping damaged magic users get back on their feet. First Axel and now Suki. "Suki can get support from me and channel her energy into the smooth running of Cloven Hoof."

"You're going to put Suki behind the bar?"

"Definitely not, I value my expensive bottles of alcohol. She has assets that will be useful. It will help her come out of her shell and learn that being sociable isn't a bad thing. Not everyone wants to poke fun at her and be mean."

Dazielle tilted her head. "What have you got in mind?"

"Leave the details to me. I'm happy to help if she's put on probation."

Dazielle jabbed a finger at me. "If I do this, you have complete responsibility for her actions. If Suki messes up or breaks the law, it lands on your head. You have to guarantee me that you'll look after her and keep her out of trouble."

"I assure you, Suki coming to work with me will be the best thing that's happened to both of us."

Dazielle smirked, the glimmer in her eyes suggesting she hoped it was a spectacular failure and I'd end up in her cells again. "I'll get the paperwork drawn up, but I'll be keeping a close eye on both of you. One mistake, and you'll both be back here."

I smiled as I turned away from the desk. Dazielle could threaten all she liked, but it looked like I had a new member of staff, and I was happy about it.

"Wait! If you stick around for a bit, I can discharge Suki into your care."

"I can't right now. I'll sign whatever needs signing later." I needed to spend some time figuring out what was niggling me about Rachel's arrest and the fight she'd had with Jenny.

I had to be certain this was all Rachel's doing and I wasn't missing something. Something that could put everyone I loved in Willow Tree Falls at risk.

Chapter 20

As I headed back along the main street with Wiggles, I saw Jenny hopping into the back of the van parked outside Unicorn's Trough, her arms full of equipment.

I hurried over and poked my head inside. The van's interior was kitted out with banks of screens and filming equipment, along with cameras and microphones.

She looked over and gasped before smiling. "Hi, Tempest, you startled me."

"I'm surprised to see you working." I looked at her hands, which were covered in a light gauze bandage.

"Oh, I feel great. I don't know what they do at that hospital of yours, but I'm almost as good as new. Besides, I need to get the last few bits sorted before we leave. James won't be happy if the work isn't completed."

"He's the slave driver making you work while your hands are healing?"

"Of course," Jenny said. "What's a girl to do? I need a job, and he's offering one. When we get out of here and things settle down, I'll look around for something else. I'm not sure journalism is for me anymore."

"It seems you do need a mean streak to be in journalism and make it to the top."

"Tell me about it. I've had enough of being bossed around by super-egos." She closed the lid of the box she was sorting through. "How's Rachel doing?"

"I haven't seen her since yesterday. I hear she's being charged with Nick's murder, so she's probably miserable."

Jenny stopped tidying the equipment and hopped out the back of the van. "Wow! So, it really was her. I can't say I'm surprised. If you're looking for a person with a mean streak, she'd be front and center of the pack."

I studied Jenny carefully. She seemed in remarkably good health after the fight. "Rachel keeps talking about this crazy theory she has."

Jenny smiled. "What theory is that?"

"She keeps talking about a bewitched ring. She said that's what sent her over the edge and why she attacked you." That wasn't true. I hadn't spoken to Rachel since the angels took her, but Jenny didn't need to know that.

Jenny's laugh sounded startled. "A bewitched ring. Are we in Narnia?"

I shrugged and forced a smile. "It's so weird. I was wondering if it was an antique ring she'd lost or wanted to buy."

Jenny stepped closer. "This ring sounds interesting. Did you get a look at it?"

"I pulled it off her finger when she was caught."

"You've got the ring?" Jenny grabbed hold of my arm. Her fingers dug into my flesh. "Where is it?"

My eyebrows rose slowly. "Why the interest?"

Jenny's eyes gleamed. "It's mine. She took it from me."

I feigned surprise as my pulse raced. "A second ago, you were surprised to learn about a ring. Are you certain it's yours?"

Jenny licked her lips. "I forgot. I mean, with everything that's been going on, it's been a stressful week. Nick dying, me being attacked by Rachel. But I'm certain she stole that ring. It belongs to me. Give it back."

"I wish I could. It was taken away."

Jenny scowled at me. "The police have it?"

"It's in a safe place. Besides, it's evidence. It can't be handed over to anyone for a while."

"But it's mine," Jenny whined.

"If it is, you'll get it back."

Jenny's smile looked forced as she let go of my arm. "Of course, I'm just curious about what sent Rachel so crazy. My ring can't have done that. I should go get it, though. I don't want it to go missing. You hear stories of corrupt police stealing precious items and selling them."

"I don't think our police will do that."

Jenny took a step away from the van, her gaze going in the direction of Angel Force's headquarters. "Even so, I need to be sure."

"Give it a couple of weeks and you can get it."

"I can't wait a couple of weeks!"

My eyes narrowed. "Why not?"

Jenny looked down at the bandages on her hands and shook her head. "I just... well, it has sentimental value."

"Is that all? Rachel is as adamant as you that it belongs to her."

"She's lying!" Jenny crossed her arms over her chest. "Maybe that's it. Nick must have found my ring and given it to Rachel. He demanded it back when he realized what an awful human being she is. They fought, and she killed him. There you go. Rachel has another reason for wanting Nick dead."

"I think we have enough reasons for that," I said. "Why would Nick give your ring to someone else?"

Jenny shrugged. "He was nice but dumb. He'd have done anything to stop Rachel's whining for five minutes. He could have found my ring and offered it to Rachel to keep her happy. He wouldn't have known it belonged to me." She took another step away.

I grabbed hold of her arm. "You probably don't want to do that."

She glared at me. "What do you mean?"

"I mean, you don't want to go anywhere near that ring ever again. You were wearing it when you fought with Rachel, weren't you?"

Her eyes widened. "How do you know that?"

"I wondered why your hands were so badly scratched. Rachel tore at your fingers because she wanted the ring." Which meant Jenny had worn the ring and experienced its powers first-hand. When a non-magical was exposed to that much power, it never ended well.

Jenny shook my hand off her arm and stepped toward me. "Do you know what this ring can do? Do you know its power?"

"A little, and you clearly do. That's why you fought with Rachel to keep it."

"I don't know what you're talking about." Jenny glanced around the street. She grabbed me by the throat and slung me with surprising force into the back of the van, before jumping on top of me and pinning me down. The van door slammed shut behind us, trapping Wiggles outside and me very much inside and in trouble.

Yikes, Jenny was strong. She must have residual magic flowing through her, thanks to wearing the demon possessed ring. And when I say residual, I mean a ton of strong, spiky, nasty feeling magic that oozed from her pores like yesterday's whiskey.

"You will tell me where the ring is," she spat in my face. "It's mine. I have a right to wear it."

"You have a right to nothing." I gasped as her fingers tightened around my throat. "That ring is not for you. It's not for anyone to use."

She slammed my head onto the floor of the van. "I will have it back. It claimed me. We are one."

I tried to lift my hands and cast a spell, but they felt heavy and slow as if the throb of Jenny's power drained me. "How long have you had the ring?"

"It claimed me after Nick found it. He discovered it the first night we were here. He was so excited that he couldn't help but tell me all about it. At first, I thought he was joking. Then he showed me the ring, and it was as if nothing else mattered. Before I realized what I was doing, I'd pulled it from his hand and slipped it on my finger." Jenny let out a contented sigh, and her eyes glazed over.

"He wasn't happy about that?"

Her expression hardened. "Nick pulled the ring off my finger. He told me not to mess with it and I didn't know what I was doing. He was an idiot. Nick had no clue what he was dealing with. That ring didn't want him; it wanted me. I knew the second the warm metal touched my flesh that we were meant to be joined."

"Joined to a piece of unnaturally warm metal that made you desire it. That didn't make you think something was off?"

She thumped my head onto the floor again. "You have no idea what you're talking about. Give me my ring."

My head ached, and my vision blurred. A sign that Frank wanted in on the action would be perfect, but he refused to show. He must still be licking his wounds from his last encounter with this power. "Did you have that ring when you came to Cloven Hoof? That was how you got in?"

Her expression grew puzzled. "Of course, I could get into your stupid bar. What's that got to do with anything?"

That was one mystery solved. There was nothing wrong with the magic barrier around Cloven Hoof. It was simply that Jenny had possession of a magic artifact, which meant she could walk through my barrier.

Finally, Frank stirred inside me as black dots flashed in front of my eyes. "It's about time."

"Time for what?" Jenny cocked her head. Her eyes blazed. "Oh! I knew there was something strange about you. I sensed it when you questioned me after Nick's death. You have power too."

"I don't have much say over this particular ability." I sensed Frank wanted to defend himself against Jenny, but something stopped him. His hot energy slid up my spine but stopped halfway and sank down. I couldn't hear him in my head. It was as if she sucked power from us both.

I heard Wiggles barking outside the van and crashing into the side as he tried to get in.

Jenny bashed my head on the floor one more time. "Now I know the ring is safe, I can find it and be reunited with it. You cannot tell anybody about this."

"I won't say a word. I've already forgotten what we were talking about."

She raised a hand above my head, a snarl on her face.

The back door of the van was yanked open. "What's going on in here?" It was James. I'd never been so happy to see his smug face.

Jenny glanced at him and shook her head. "Leave us alone."

"Jenny, what are you doing to Tempest?" He ignored her advice and clambered into the back of the van. Wiggles was right behind him, his hackles raised and his eyes glowing as he saw Jenny on top of me.

I gestured for Wiggles to keep back. "You really do need to get lost," I gasped at James. If he got between two magic users fighting, he'd be toast.

James's ego was not paying attention to the danger he'd wandered into. "I don't know what this is, but you both need to stop."

"You always were a jerk." Jenny flicked a hand toward him. James flew backwards out of the van and landed on the ground.

"Wiggles, keep him out of this," I yelled.

Wiggles stared at me for a second before jumping on top of James's chest and pinning him down.

Our fight had drawn the attention of others, who must have sensed the dark magic exuding from Jenny. Several worried-looking faces peered in at us.

Brogan appeared and stared down at James. When Brogan raised his head, his eyes glowed a liquid silver as he saw Jenny on top of me. His fingers sparked with magic. "Ladies, this fight must end."

Jenny eased her hold on me a fraction as she gazed at the growing crowd behind the van. She rolled off me, and her eyes widened in mock fear. "I'm innocent. I have nothing to do with this. She attacked me." She pointed a shaking finger in my direction as I struggled to my feet and rubbed my sore throat.

"That's not true," I said. "Jenny's had her hands on the Ring of Halo for days. It's changed her."

"You know nothing about me or my ring," she hissed.

"What on earth is going on?" James protested from the ground. "Will somebody get this dog off me? I think it has fleas, and it's drooling on my shirt."

"Wiggles, don't let him up," I called. It was too late to stop James from seeing what we really were. He was surrounded by magic users who weren't being too careful about hiding their powers as they sensed the danger from Jenny. Before James left Willow Tree Falls, he'd need another mind wipe.

"I insist, or I'm calling the police and animal control." James squirmed until Wiggles caught hold of the front of his shirt in his teeth and snarled at him.

"That's enough." Brogan reached down and touched Wiggles. "He is involved now."

Wiggles looked at me, and I shrugged. James was in for a shock. I hoped he could handle it.

James struggled up and brushed dirt from the back of his pants, his cautious gaze on Wiggles, who remained alert by the back of the van, his attention fixed to me. "Why are you fighting with each other?"

"It's her," Jenny said. "She's claiming I'm involved with Nick's murder when we all know it was Rachel."

James looked from me to Jenny. "Is this true? I thought Rachel had been charged. The whole sorry mess is over, and I have all the information I need for my exclusive."

"The police have the wrong person," I said.

James laughed. "You think it was Jenny? She can't have anything to do with this."

"You see? I have a witness to prove my innocence," Jenny said. "I had nothing to do with Nick's death in the cemetery."

"He wasn't killed in the cemetery, though, was he? Nick was killed inside the standing stones and his body moved." I looked around the inside of the van, recalling Suki mentioning hearing an engine noise near the stones. "He was probably moved using this van, a van Jenny knows well since she uses it as her mobile office."

"What nonsense," Jenny said. "Other people use this van. I'm not strong enough to kill anybody."

"You would if you had possession of the Ring of Halo."

"The ring of what?" James asked, his eyes gleaming with the promise of a story to tantalize his readers.

"Never mind," I said. "Jenny killed Nick and moved him. It was all because of this ring."

"I'm not admitting to anything," Jenny said. "You have no proof I was involved."

"Hold on. If it's proof you need, I can show it to you," James said.

"How can you do that?" I asked.

"Easy. When we first got here, I rigged a fixed camera at the standing stones. I wanted twenty-four-hour footage of the place. Sometimes, you get funny shots or interesting pictures of wildlife. More often than not, though, the cameras simply catch couples making out in the dark, thinking no one can see them. All that footage has its uses."

My heartbeat kicked up a gear. "You've recorded everything that happened at the stones?"

"Everything. And it's all time stamped."

"You won't find anything." Jenny sounded frantic as she blocked access to the equipment.

"If we won't find anything, then it doesn't matter if we take a look," I said.

"No, I mean, you won't see me doing anything." Jenny's panicked gaze looked around at the growing crowd of people behind the van. "I'm innocent."

"Sure you are." I gestured to James. "Show us the footage."

James grinned, seeming happy to be the center of attention despite the bizarre circumstances. He hopped into the back of the van and sidled past Jenny.

She lunged at the equipment and grabbed a laptop. I was ready for her this time. I wrapped my arms around her and flooded her with calming magic. It took effort, and I was trembling by the time the spell had an effect, but Jenny lowered the laptop and slumped in my arms.

James looked at me, alarm clear in his eyes. "What did you do to her?"

"It's a bit like a Vulcan death grip. Squeeze a person in the right place, and they pass out. Get the footage up." I lowered Jenny onto a seat and pinned her down with magic.

James was still staring at me when I turned back around. "You are the oddest person I've ever met."

"It won't be the first time someone's told me that." I gestured at the bank of equipment. "The footage?"

He glanced at the crowd outside the van. "Very well." James spent a moment bringing up files and checking through them. "This is the one. I fixed the camera on top of one of those old stones."

"You do realize how important those stones are," Brogan grumbled, his eyes still gleaming silver as his magic lurked beneath the surface.

"It's a bit of old rock," James said. "I didn't do it any harm when I climbed on it."

I raised a hand to Brogan as he approached the van, his fists clenched. Now wasn't the right time to sucker punch James. Later, definitely later. Those stones were sacred to Willow Tree Falls, and no one got to climb on them.

"Bring up the footage from just after midnight on the night Nick was murdered," I instructed.

James scrolled through the footage for a few minutes.

"Wait, go back a bit." I'd spotted a lone figure come into the camera's view.

James muttered under his breath, something about him not being my slave, but I chose to ignore him.

I watched as Nick appeared and wandered around the stones, slipping in and out of sight.

"What was he playing at?" James said. "I hope he wasn't trying to get a story over me."

"He won't be getting anything over you," I snapped. "He's dead, remember?"

James huffed and shoved his hands into his pockets. "I remember. I'm the one being forced to write his memorial message in the blasted paper."

"Make sure you do a good job." I kept my gaze fixed on the laptop screen. I tensed as I saw Nick standing alone and a figure run up behind him. They jumped him and whacked him over the back of the head.

James sucked in a breath and leaned closer to the screen.

"Come on. I need to see your face," I whispered as I continued to watch the footage.

"I thought Nick died in the cemetery?" James said.

"It doesn't look like it," I said. We scrolled through the footage, stopping it again when the back of a van appeared in the camera's view. The killer ran to Nick's body and dragged him toward the van. I still hadn't seen their face, so I couldn't be sure it was Jenny.

As they got closer to the van, the killer stumbled and fell backward. The hood they wore came off, revealing Jenny's dark hair.

James gasped and looked over at Jenny. "She's the killer? What about Rachel?"

"Rachel is innocent," I said.

James rubbed his forehead, and a smile spread across his face. "This is brilliant. I thought I was here to cover a story about the solstice, and I've got an exclusive on a murder." He glanced at me. "And I want to talk to you. There's something off about you."

"I have no story to tell you."

"You're involved in this. Maybe this isn't a love triangle between Nick, Rachel, and Jenny but a love square. Are you also in love with Nick?"

"Wiggles, Brogan, can you deal with this problem?" I gestured at James.

"Our pleasure." Wiggles grabbed James by the ankle as Brogan wrapped a hand around James's arm and yanked him from the van.

James yelped and disappeared from view.

"Is everything okay in here?" Rhett poked his head inside the van. His eyes widened as he saw Jenny slumped in a seat.

"It will be. Can you message Angel Force and tell them to haul their feathered butts over here? They've charged the wrong person with Nick's murder."

Concern flashed in Rhett's eyes. "Of course. Are you okay?"

I nodded as I slumped against the side of the van. "I will be." All I needed was a week in bed with a stack of cupcakes, and I'd be just perfect.

Chapter 21

It had been two days since Jenny had been revealed as Nick's killer, and everything finally felt back to normal.

I stretched out on the large checked picnic blanket in the cemetery and smiled as I took in the scene around me. Everyone was there. Mom handed out sandwiches, Aurora sat with Auntie Queenie and Uncle Kenny in the shade of a tree, Granny Dottie and Grandpa Lucius debated whether clotted cream or double cream went best with strawberries, and Wiggles was off bounding around the gravestones chasing butterflies. I was happy to be surrounded by it all.

Mom handed me a glass of something sparkling. "Don't worry. It's not alcoholic. It's sparkling apple juice. You deserve a treat after your hard work finding Nick's killer."

"And for clearing my name," Auntie Queenie said as she peered out at me from under the brim of a large purple hat, a pastry in one hand.

"That was tough," I said. "I really thought you'd end up behind bars. Maybe be more discreet when you make your threats to journalists. And no more mention of demon sacrifices."

Auntie Queenie had the decency to look embarrassed. "It was a little joke. Who would actually believe I'd do such a thing?"

"What's going to happen to Jenny?" Aurora asked.

"Angel Force has seen the footage, and she's been charged with murder. They're holding her until they can figure out what to do with a non-magical who broke our laws. She will need special treatment. They can hardly shove her in a demon prison and expect her to thrive."

"She deserves it," Granny Dottie said. "She caused a lot of trouble here."

"Nick started it," I said. "With his magic ancestral roots and him discovering information about the Ring of Halo, he started this hunt and ended up putting a lot of people at risk."

"It's a shame it ended in his death," Mom said. "We've got the ring tucked away in the house, so no one can get to it. The sooner it's back where it belongs, the better. And we need to be quick. Your gran has been dropping hints about trying it on."

I shuddered. Granny Dottie caused enough trouble without having a dark magic ring jammed on her finger. "Suki is having a few days off before she gets back to her forest duties. She found the recent events overwhelming. I'll be keeping a close eye on her." I took a sip of the apple juice. "In fact, I was thinking of offering her a part-time job at Cloven Hoof. I've got to watch out for her, so she keeps her nose clean and doesn't punch any more angels."

Granny Dottie snorted a laugh. "Punching angels, what fun."

"What sort of job can Suki do for you?" Grandpa Lucius asked as he glanced affectionately at his wife.

"I was thinking a bouncer," I said.

Aurora smiled. "Oh, yes! That will be perfect. She's intimidating to look at. Anyone who wants to cause trouble at the door will think twice when they run into Suki."

"Exactly. I haven't officially asked her yet, but it will do her good and give her a chance to socialize more. She must get lonely in the forest. I also need to get the word out that she wants an apprentice. Managing the forest on her own is too much for one wood nymph, even more so if she's going to spend time at Cloven Hoof."

"I can put a note up in Heaven's Door," Aurora said. "I'm sure we'll find someone lovely to assist her."

"Thanks, I'll do the same at the other stores," I said.

"We need to look after Suki," Mom said. "It must be hard being alone and scared of what other people think of her. When she's ready, we'll invite her around for dinner and discuss her job prospects."

I grinned at Mom. "It's going to take a while before she can handle dinner with all of us."

Mom tutted and clipped me around the head.

"I saw that other journalist and the rude non-magical woman scurrying out of here yesterday," Granny Dottie said. "I'm glad to see the back of them."

I nodded as I accepted a huge plate of sandwiches from Mom. "So did I. I got the impression Rachel has latched onto James as her next conquest. He's too confused to know what's going on. I had to do another mind wipe on him after he saw everything. He's a stubborn one and doesn't let go of a story easily. With a bit of luck, he'll write the most boring story about us imaginable. No one will want to come here after they've read his article."

"I was thinking it would be nice to do something to remember Nick," Aurora said. "We can have a little plaque or something in the cemetery as a way to remember him. He did mess up in his hunt for the Ring of Halo, but it wasn't his fault. It was his natural curiosity that killed him."

"It was a magic crazed woman with a rock in her hand that did that," Granny Dottie said.

Aurora tutted at her. "Don't you think it would be nice, though? We can keep it discreet."

"That's a lovely idea," Mom said. "Maybe we can have something we can put flowers in, as well."

I nodded as I munched on a smoked salmon and cream cheese sandwich. It felt good to be surrounded by my family. It would be so easy to get used to this and think I could stay here all the time. Despite Frank's recent efforts to get free, he wasn't happy, and I knew I'd need to leave again soon. Frank needed a proper day out, and Willow Tree Falls was not the place to do that.

Aurora shuffled over and joined me on the blanket. She snaffled a sandwich from my plate, and we ate together in silence for a few minutes.

"I feel like I've hardly seen you," she said quietly. "When I do, I've had to run away before you throttled me. And I know you're going away again."

My shrug was apologetic. "How do you know that?"

"Dazielle was in Heaven's Door and said you've accepted a new job from her."

I frowned. Dazielle talked too much. "I'll be back."

"We've barely spent any safe time together."

"There's a good reason for that," I said. "Plus, I got my arm twisted in helping to solve this murder."

"I know, but next time you come back, let's see if we can't figure out a way to hang out more without Frank causing us problems." She nudged me as she stole another sandwich. "I miss you."

I stared up into the sky and repressed a sigh. I'd love that. I'd love to hang out with my sister all the time, but even her sitting next to me had perked Frank's attention. "I'm sure we can do something."

"Great. Maybe we can have a girlie day at the spa. It's been awhile since I've been in the thermal waters."

"I'm not sure about a girlie day."

"How about a girlie morning?"

"Maybe not a girlie anything."

Aurora pouted at me. "I can come demon hunting with you. You can teach me all about the non-magical world on the other side of the barrier."

"Nope, out of the question," I said. "When I'm out of Willow Tree Falls, Frank is much more prevalent. If you spend time with me in the land of non-magicals, he will eat you alive."

Aurora shifted on the blanket and eyed me with caution. "Well, I don't want that. Maybe we won't do demon hunting together."

"Good plan. We will do something, though. I promise."

"Since you're about to leave us, I got you two going away presents." Aurora grinned at me and sat up.

"You've never done that before." My gaze narrowed as I saw the wicked smile on her face. "What have you done?"

She pointed over my head. "They're arriving now."

I turned my head, and my heart skipped a beat. Rhett and Axel strode through the gates of the cemetery toward us.

I groaned and closed my eyes for a second. "Why did you invite them both?"

"Oh, come off it. You like them. There's no harm in them coming here and enjoying some of the food Mom's spent hours preparing."

"Ooooh, gorgeous men to enjoy." Granny Dottie chuckled and smoothed her skirt over her knees.

"This day keeps getting better."

Mom grabbed two more plates. "I made extra. I know how growing boys like to eat."

I glared at her. "You knew about this?"

Mom shared a smile with Aurora. "I might have known something about it." She hopped up and hugged Rhett and Axel. "Welcome to the picnic. There's plenty for everyone, so don't be shy about helping yourselves."

"Thanks, Mrs. Crypt," Rhett said as he smiled at me.

"None of that Mrs. anything. It's Cora."

Rhett nodded, and Axel smiled at my mom, his grin so bright it dazzled me.

After they'd loaded their plates with food, they looked around for somewhere to sit. Aurora hopped up from the blanket. "There's plenty of room for the two of you on here. I need to stretch my legs."

"Don't leave me alone," I whispered to her.

All Aurora did was wink at me and skip away like the treacherous, matchmaking fool she was.

Rhett and Axel looked as uncomfortable as I felt as they squashed themselves onto the blanket.

I smiled at them, trying to ignore how mortified I felt by being so obviously set up by my entire family.

"It sounds like you've been having quite an adventure," Axel said. "A dead journalist, an enchanted ring, and a fight with a crazed non-magical."

"Tempest handled herself just fine," Rhett said.

Axel glared at him. "I never said she didn't."

"It's all dealt with now. The dangerous magic is contained, the killer has been arrested, and all the journalists have vanished." I did not like the whiff of alpha dog building between these two. I would not be fought over like a piece of prime steak.

"When will one of you fine young men ask for my granddaughter's hand in marriage?" Granny Dottie asked.

I cringed and glared at her. "Ignore her. We think she's losing her marbles. She says all sorts of ridiculous things."

Granny Dottie frowned at me. "Less of your lip."

Rhett and Axel grinned as I looked at them. "Don't you dare indulge her. She's trying to stir up trouble."

"It's not a terrible idea," Axel said.

Rhett frowned at him. "You want to marry Tempest?"

Axel shrugged. "Well, I have to settle down sometime."

"Thanks! I'm not settling for anyone," I said.

Axel's cheeks flushed. "I didn't mean that. I meant I wouldn't be settling if I picked you."

"You're assuming I'm interested in settling. I might like being single."

"It gets boring," Auntie Queenie said, clearly listening in to the conversation. "Find yourself a handsome stud and enjoy yourself. Remember what we talked about?" She nodded her head vigorously at Rhett and Axel.

"What did you talk about?" Rhett asked.

"Nothing important. Auntie Queenie has strange theories when it comes to controlling Frank. All of it is nonsense." There was no way I'd tell Rhett and Axel Auntie Queenie's theory about having lots of sex to keep control of her magic and reduce stress.

Rhett smirked as he ate a mini quiche.

My cheeks flushed. "Just to be clear, I'm not in the arena for marriage."

"Are you in the arena for dating?" Rhett asked.

"You should choose the one with the motorbike," Granny Dottie said. "I like his stubble. And anyone who knows how to control such a powerful machine has got to have strong muscles. Can I feel your biceps, Rhett?"

"Please, don't show her your biceps," I said to Rhett. "She'll get overexcited, and her heart will give out."

He laughed. "Sorry, Dottie, I haven't been to the gym in a while. There's nothing to feel."

"There's no need to be shy," Granny Dottie said. "Any time you want someone to ride pillion with you, you only have to say the word. I have my own helmet."

Grandpa Lucius patted her knee. "I'll take you for a ride, old girl, so long as you behave yourself."

"Less of the old." Granny Dottie stroked his cheek affectionately.

"If you're into bikes, I'm restoring a classic at the moment," Axel said. "I think I'd look great in a set of leathers."

"It takes more than leathers to make a biker," Rhett muttered.

I shook my head. It wasn't about the bikes or the leathers, although they were kind of sexy. I discreetly studied both men as they continued to eat and banter with Granny Dottie. They had their charms but also had things that made me realize it wouldn't be a good idea to date either of them. I had to keep reminding myself that I wasn't looking for a date. And I wasn't looking for a date with any bad boys.

Still, they were tempting. If I could figure out how to squash Frank for a few weeks and really get to know them both, things could be different. I could make a decision and find a guy who would put up with me and my annoying demon.

Wiggles raced over to the blanket. He snatched a sandwich out of Axel's hand and gave him a dirty look before bounding away again.

Axel shook his head. "I'm telling you that dog does not like me."

"He's got good taste," Rhett said.

The ground beneath us rumbled. Everyone was instantly alert.

"That felt like a new crack in the prison." Mom was on her feet, her hands already sparking with magic.

Granny Dottie stood. "Let's see what the problem is. Don't worry everyone. You carry on with the picnic. We've got a little demon problem to deal with. We'll be back in time for cake." Defying her years, she sprinted away with Mom, magic crackling off both of them as they hunted for the crack and the sneaky demon trying to break out.

I reclined back on the blanket, knowing Mom and Granny Dottie would keep us safe. Aurora sat next to me on the grass, and we watched our incredible family as they hunted for demons and ensured the rest of the world remained safe.

"Our family is awesome," Aurora said.

I gave her hand a quick squeeze. She was right. I might be leaving soon, but I had everything to come back for.

About Author

K.E. O'Connor (Karen) is a cozy mystery author living in the beautiful British countryside. She loves all things mystery, animals, and cake (these feature in her books.)

When she's not writing about mysteries, murder, and treats, she volunteers at a local animal sanctuary, reads a ton of books, binge watches mystery series on TV, and dreams about living somewhere warmer.

To stay in touch with the fun mysteries, where the killer always gets caught, justice is served magic style, and the familiars talk, join her newsletter.

Newsletter:
www.subscribepage.com/cozymysteries
Website: www.keoconnor.com/writing
Facebook: www.facebook.com/keoconnorauthor

Also By

Luck of the Witch

Hell of a Witch

Revenge of the Witch

Curse of the Witch

Son of a Witch

Framing of the Witch

Trickery of the Witch

Wishes of the Witch

Harmony of the Witch

Remedy of the Witch

Gift of the Witch

Toil of the Witch

Jinxing of the Witch

Craving of the Witch

Union of the Witch

Chaos of the Witch

Sleighing of the Witch

If you enjoyed

Hell of a Witch

turn the page to read an extract from the next Crypt
Witch Mystery

REVENGE OF THE WITCH

ISBN: 978-1-915378-01-9

Chapter 1

"There's one of the little imps!" My sister, Aurora Crypt, pointed to a sickly green vapor as it slid from a crack in the cemetery.

I shook my head. Only Aurora would call a potentially lethal, soul sucking demon an imp.

"I'm on it." I raced over, stick in hand, and slammed it on the head of the demon who was trying to escape the prison.

"There's another creeping through here," Aurora yelled.

As I turned, she slammed her own stick on top of a demon's horned head before sealing the crack with a blast of white magic.

It was unusual for me to work a shift at the cemetery, but the resident demons were being tricky. They'd been disrupting the stability of the prison for almost a week, launching relentless attacks on any weakness they discovered. The whole family was working overtime to ensure none of them crept out and caused chaos.

The sticks we held weren't your average sticks, but powerful magic staffs that weakened demons by absorbing their energy when they came into contact with them.

"This is like a game of whack a mole, just with demons." Wiggles, my mostly faithful talking hellhound, wandered over with a stick in his mouth. This stick was for throwing, not smacking down misbehaving demons.

I checked the coast was clear before throwing the stick for him. I turned at the sound of a teeth jarring crack and saw Aurora slam a demon back down. For a witch who followed the white magic path, she sure looked thrilled to be pounding demons.

She wiped a hand across her forehead and grinned at me. "What's going on with these guys? They've got a bee in their twisted demon bonnets about something."

"Maybe they've stopped bitching at each other and decided it's better to work together to break out of our prison. Not that it will do them any good."

"Not when we're here with our fancy twirlers." Aurora spun the stick in her hand like a talented majorette.

I did the same, and the stick landed with a thud on the ground. "Whatever their plans are, we'll stop them."

"Over there! Here comes another one." Aurora pointed over my shoulder.

I raced in the direction of a red mist covering part of the cemetery.

"Tempest, this does not look good," Aurora whispered as she joined me, her fingers digging into my arm. "You know what a red mist means."

"That we won't get any freshly baked muffins from this demon," I said. Demons had different ways of emerging. Some appeared in a cloud of purple mist. Others favored green, but the ones you needed to worry about the most came with a red or black tinge. It promised twisted, nasty magic. Magic that burned your skin and threatened to send you mad if you spent any time immersed in it. That kind of evil was never permitted to run loose in our cemetery.

"We should call for backup," Aurora said. "Mom and Granny Dottie have more experience with this kind of demon."

The mist curled toward us as I raised my stick. "We don't need them. We've learned from the best."

Aurora adjusted the stick in her hand. "Are you sure?"

"Would your big sister ever lie to you?"

"You do about food."

I glanced at her out of the corner of my eye. "When have I ever lied about food?"

"At my eighth birthday party, when the chocolate cupcakes went missing. I knew you'd taken them, but you swore to Mom you hadn't."

"I don't remember that." Those cupcakes had been amazing. Rich and gooey and covered in popping candy. I'd eaten two every night for a week until they were too stale, sneaking the wrappers off and hiding under my covers as I read my book by torchlight. It was heaven.

"You do! I found the moldy wrappers under your bed."

I turned my full attention to Aurora. "You know better than to look under my bed."

Aurora huffed out a breath. "My friends thought I'd lied about those cupcakes."

"It didn't ruin the party. And you're still the most popular girl in Willow Tree Falls, even if you are too stingy to serve cupcakes at your birthday."

"Tempest!" Aurora glared at me. "Those were my party cupcakes."

I tapped my stick in my hand. "We can't focus on cupcakes. This demon smells like Baccaras. Do you remember him? I dragged him here after almost a month of searching. He stank so bad I had to burn my clothes."

Aurora sniffed the air and gagged. "Sulfur, rotten fish, and... what else is it?"

"I always thought he stank like used diapers."

"Yes! That's it. Baccaras smells of a soggy diaper." Aurora grinned at me. "We can handle him together."

Witches and demons were never close friends. There were a number of half-demons living in Willow Tree Falls, but the full-on demons were too chaotic to be trusted. They had lifetime bans unless they got a never-get-out-of-jail card from me.

Even though I hosted a particularly unpleasant demon, Frank, inside me in order to keep my sister safe, I had little time for them. When I wasn't in Willow Tree Falls, I was out capturing misbehaving demons and bringing them into Angel Force to deal with.

The ground trembled beneath our feet. It was a sure sign the demon was on his way.

We stood in an attack stance, sticks raised and knees bent, ready to swipe his head if he dared pop his horns out for a sniff of fresh air.

"Are you sure it's Baccaras?" Aurora whispered.

I shook my head. There were thousands of demons beneath our feet. I hadn't captured them all. Some had been here for hundreds of years, maybe longer. Monitoring the demon prison had been the family business for centuries. That's what the Crypt family did. We kept the rest of the world safe from devious demons.

The ground rumbled again, and a spurt of steam shot from a new crack.

"We should seal the crack before he comes through." Aurora stepped forward.

I grabbed her arm. "This demon needs to be taught a lesson. Try to escape our prison, and you end up with a bad headache and your power drained."

I glanced over my shoulder and was relieved to see Wiggles engrossed in chewing his stick. It was a habit he'd never had when he was a regular dog. Turn him into a hellhound and he developed a love of all things sticky. I didn't want Wiggles anywhere near a demon. Even though he was a hellhound and had a hide as tough as a rhino, they still might like to play with him.

My hand went to my stomach as Frank stirred. He'd been quiet these past three hours since I'd started working with Aurora, but I was taking a chance being around her for so long. Frank loved Aurora. Or rather, Frank would love to kill Aurora.

I stifled a sulfurous belch behind my hand as Frank's energy pulsed strongly. I took two steps away from Aurora. I didn't want her worrying about me when we had a demon trying to break free.

"Stay where you are," I muttered to Frank.

"Your charming sister is so close. I can smell her. What do you expect me to do?" His voice was just a whisper in my head.

"Slide out of me and head into the prison, like you're supposed to do." Frank was a stubborn son of a demon. All my attempts to get him out of me had failed. It seemed he liked living inside a witch.

"Where's the fun in that? If I was in there, I couldn't enjoy your fascinating company."

I snorted, and my fingers tightened around the stick. I'd get rid of Frank one day and finally be rid of his sweet tooth, bad attitude, and twisted desire to choke the life from my only sister.

"Here he comes," Aurora yelled as the red mist intensified and a low hissing emerged from the crack.

"Are you ready?" I asked her as the mist stung my eyes and blurred my vision.

She nodded, her blue eyes wide but a determined look on her face. "We've got this."

"It's time for a game of whack a demon." Wiggles trotted over.

"Don't get involved," I cautioned him. "You don't want to be dragged into the prison."

Wiggles cocked his head. "You'd come and get me if that happened."

"Sorry, buddy. You'd be on your own if you were dumb enough to get caught by a demon." I probably would get him out, but I wouldn't enjoy it.

Wiggles squinted up at me, his eyes glowing their usual hellhound red. "They'd love me down there. I'd fit right in."

I had to smile. He was right. Wiggles had a way of charming everybody, and now that he came with a nifty side order of hellhound, the demons wouldn't mind him at all. But Wiggles was my best friend, and no demon was getting its mean little claws on him.

I coughed as the mist grew thicker and swiped my hand across my face, so I wouldn't miss the moment the demon emerged.

"Do you see him?" Aurora yelled.

"I can barely see where you are," I said. "You?"

"Nothing yet. I'll get closer."

"Don't risk it," I yelled. "We'll know when he's here."

The ground bucked, and there was a ripping sound of stone grinding together as the crack grew larger.

I drew the stick over my head and inched closer. Any second now, the demon would poke his head out, and he'd be sorry when he did.

"Be careful of this one," Frank whispered in my head. "He likes to eat feisty witches for dinner."

"He can keep his demon paws off us," I muttered. "He's not getting to play tonight."

"Don't say I didn't warn you," Frank said.

That was an odd thing about Frank. Although his singular mission was to get free and attack Aurora, he came in handy now and again. His powers were wild and unpredictable, but when he gained control, there was little that could beat us. We were a weird and inappropriate double act.

I appreciated it when Frank's energy faded. Although he was a pain in the backside, he tended not to cause me much trouble when I needed to focus. I sometimes felt he was looking out for me, but that wasn't possible. Frank was chaos and evil. He was no-one's friendly uncle.

I grabbed a nearby headstone to stop from falling as the ground rumbled under my feet again.

"I think I see him," Aurora shouted. "Over here."

"Where's here?" I let go of the headstone and stumbled through the thick, sour smelling mist.

Aurora screamed, and I increased my pace, heading in the direction of the sound.

My eyes widened as I saw an enormous head, topped with black curling horns, jutting out of the crack in the ground. The crack had spread several yards across the cemetery, and Aurora stood at the opposite end to me, swiping her stick at the demon as his clawed arm flew through the air trying to reach her.

"No, you don't." I raced over and slammed my stick into the back of the demon's head repeatedly.

He roared but was unable to turn, given the tightness of the gap he was in. But he was inching his way out, and I did not want to see the rest of his enormous bulk come out of that crack.

Aurora joined the attack, and between us, we jabbed and poked, enraging him as he spat sharp shards of brimstone at us.

"It's working," Aurora yelled. "He's getting smaller. We're taking his energy."

I squinted at the demon. He was getting smaller, but he was also pulsing. That was a bad sign. "We should get back."

"We've almost got him," Aurora said. "A few more whacks, and he'll be back inside."

"I think he's going to—" the demon exploded in a hot shower of sticky red goo.

A huge backdraft sucked the majority of the goo toward me as the demon slid into the crack, muttering curses in Latin.

The gross smelling goo covered me from head to toe, and I was thrown off my feet as it slammed into my face. I landed on my back with a gasp and lay there staring up at the star-filled sky.

Wiggles trotted over and looked at me before shaking his head. "What is it with you and demon goo? You enjoy bathing in the stuff."

"Not out of choice." I swiped my hand over my goo covered mouth and grimaced. Demon goo always had the underlying taste of rotten eggs and sour milk.

I sat up slowly and shook goo off my favorite black jacket. I watched as Aurora expertly sealed the crack in the demon prison, and the last of the red mist evaporated, leaving nothing but a clear night lit by a large, pale moon.

As she walked over, I let out an exasperated sigh. Aurora had escaped all the demon goo. Her white pullover and fitted dark jeans were spotless. Other than a glow to her cheeks from the exercise we'd gotten smacking the demon, she looked like she'd just stepped out of a salon.

Aurora held her hand out to me. "It's time for a shift change."

I waved away her hand, not wanting to cover her in the sticky muck I'd just been showered in.

Aurora ignored me, grabbed my arm, and helped me to my feet. "I can get that jacket clean. It's just a bit of demon residue. You've been covered in worse."

I belched again, and Frank stirred, his interest more acute after Aurora had touched me. "Auntie Queenie should be here in a moment to take over."

Aurora nodded. She knew how tricky it was for us to spend too much time together without Frank crashing the party. She wisely dropped her hold on my arm and took a few steps back. "We did a great job tonight."

I smiled at her. "We make a good team."

"Did someone say tea?" Auntie Queenie strolled over, a large bag slung over one arm and a pastry in her free hand.

Aurora hurried over and kissed her cheek. "We were saying it was almost time for you to get here."

"I'm here, right on time." She looked around the cemetery. "It seems quiet." Her gaze went to the goo splattered on me and the ground, but she didn't pass comment.

I exchanged a smile with Aurora. "We've been bored all night. Nothing to do but play cards and count stars."

Auntie Queenie sidestepped the goo as she finished her pastry. "Tempest, you get off and see how Cloven Hoof is doing. We can handle things from here."

I nodded goodbye and hurried out of the cemetery with Wiggles. My bar, Cloven Hoof, sat at the other end of Willow Tree Falls, only a ten-minute walk from the cemetery. It was a specialist bar, serving mildly magical and completely legal treats. Other than when we had the occasional party, it was a chilled-out place, and it was just where I wanted to be tonight. Hunting demons was stressful.

I headed to the front door and nodded at Suki, who stood outside.

Suki was a new recruit to Cloven Hoof. Being a giant wood nymph with muscular arms like gnarled tree trunks, she did an excellent job as an intimidating bouncer.

"How's everything going tonight?" I asked her.

Her gaze traveled over my goo splattered appearance before she nodded. "There are plenty of people in, but they're behaving themselves."

"Tempest Crypt, as I live and breathe."

I turned and stared at the three guys approaching Cloven Hoof. I groaned inwardly as I recognized Dewey Lavern, Puddle Lavern's nephew. He'd always been a smarmy git when growing up. Now that he was an adult, nothing had changed.

"Dewey, what brings you to Willow Tree Falls?" I asked him. "The last time I saw you here, you said this village was too backward for your city tastes."

"Visiting my auntie. Mom said the old girl gets lonely living in that cottage on her own." He smirked and shoved his thick, dark hair off his forehead. Some people might consider Dewey attractive, but his eyes always looked cold to me. "That's an interesting look you're wearing." His gaze ran over my ruined clothing.

I flicked goo off my hand, so it splattered on the ground by his feet. "I'm trying something new."

Dewey kicked dirt over the goo. "These are my friends, Serath Duckle and Bart Ranger. We're staying a few days. I'm showing them around my childhood home."

I nodded at the two guys with him. I'd seen them with Dewey before on his rare visits. Serath was tall and pale with large blue eyes. Bart was shorter and stockier with a stubbled chin and dark eyes that swept around as if he was looking for something.

"Even with gross goo on you, you're looking good, Tempest," Dewey said. "Are you still single?"

"As ever, just as I like it."

"We'll come to Cloven Hoof later. You can buy me a drink, and we can catch up."

"Tempest doesn't need to buy the drinks in here, buddy," Wiggles said. "She owns the place."

Dewey stared at Wiggles. "It talks."

"Well spotted." I nudged Wiggles with my calf as he growled. "Cloven Hoof might not be the place for you. You should try the Ancient Imp."

"That's where we're going now. I'll look in later when the place gets livelier."

"This is as lively as it gets. I like it that way." I shook my head as I watched them saunter away, a picture of cocky arrogance. There was no room for idiots in my life and definitely no room for Dewey Lavern and his dodgy friends.

"That guy is a jerk," Wiggles said.

I nodded. "You always were an excellent judge of character."

"I bet he's not had a date in years. He stinks of desperate loser."

"Does not dating make you a loser?"

"Absolutely." He tilted his head to look at me. "It's why I keep telling you to marry Brogan."

Suki coughed into her hand, and I saw a smile on her face as she looked away.

"Brogan Costin is part vampire."

"So?"

"So, he might like a plump little hellhound to nibble on at night. If we start dating, he could mistake you as a snack."

"Who are you calling plump?"

I laughed. "You don't mind being a vampire snack, but you mind me pointing out your pot belly?"

"I do not have a pot belly. Besides, I bite back. If Brogan decided I'd make a good hot dog, I'd soon change his mind." He gnashed his teeth together.

"Come on," I said to Wiggles. "Less talk about marrying me off. I need to get rid of this demon goo."

"Then we can have cake."

"Only if you want a bigger belly. I was thinking we can do some work behind the bar. And I've got a stack of paperwork to go through."

"But first cake," Wiggles said. "And no more talking about my belly, or I'll get a complex."

I grinned as I opened the door to Cloven Hoof and let Wiggles in. He might have a little belly, but I adored it. I did not adore him trying to hook me up with Brogan, although Brogan did make the best breakfasts in the whole of Willow Tree Falls.

I had enough on my plate without dating. Paperwork beckoned, and it seemed, so did cake if Wiggles had anything to do with it.

That's what occupied my time. Demons, paperwork, goo, and the occasional cake. That was fine by me.

Revenge of the Witch is available in paperback and e-book.

ISBN: 978-1-915378-01-9